# THE
# SUMMER
# LION

Also by Margi McAllister:

ARCHIE'S WAR

A HOME FOR TEASEL

FAWN

# THE
# SUMMER
# LION

Margi McAllister

SCHOLASTIC

First published in the UK in 2015 by Scholastic Children's Books
An imprint of Scholastic Ltd
Euston House, 24 Eversholt Street,
London, NW1 1DB, UK
Registered office: Westfield Road, Southam, Warwickshire, CV47 0RA
SCHOLASTIC and associated logos are trademarks and/or registered
trademarks of Scholastic Inc.

ISBN 978 1407 14557 0

A CIP catalogue record for this book is available from the British Library.

Printed and bound by CPI Group (UK) Ltd, Croydon, CR0 4YY
Papers used by Scholastic Children's Books are made from
wood grown in sustainable forests.

1 3 5 7 9 10 8 6 4 2

www.scholastic.co.uk

*For Matthew*

# Chapter One

On a summer evening a group of brightly painted wagons were clustered together on a hill. Walking towards them was a tall, thin man with a lion on a lead. A short, round woman and two little girls hurried across the grass to meet him.

"It's a disgrace!" cried the woman. "It's shocking, that's what it is!"

The two girls ran to the lion, but their mother stopped them.

"Sapphire, Spangle, don't touch it!" she said. "Poor old thing, it might have fleas or something!"

"They called him Samson," said the man, whose name was Freddie Snapdragon. "They only let me have him if I promised not to tell anyone where I got him from."

"They're a lot of scoundrels," said his wife. "No circus should have performing lions. Walking round the ring for show, fair enough, but lions aren't meant to do tricks. It's no way to treat a proud, strong creature. It gives circuses a bad name."

"But we're a circus," said Sapphire, the eldest girl.

"Only we've never had lions and things," said her sister Spangle.

"That's because we're the *best* circus," said her mother. "We don't have to ill-treat animals to get people to come and see us. Now we need to fill a bath to give him a good wash and find him something to eat. Poor thing, he doesn't have many teeth left."

Freddie Snapdragon looked round. "Where's Drina gone?" he asked. Nobody knew where Drina, the youngest of the Snapdragon children, had got to. She was nearly three years old and good at disappearing quickly.

"She'll be in one of the wagons, I suppose," said Freddie. "You know what she's like. I'll look for her while you do what you can for this poor old thing. And I don't like the name 'Samson'," he added. "We could change that."

The lion was left tethered to a wagon by a long rope while Mrs Snapdragon and the two older girls put cans of water to warm on the campfire. Freddie Snapdragon called from one wagon to the next, looking for his youngest daughter.

While all this was happening, a small figure appeared at the door of the Snapdragon family's wagon,

2

carrying a mug half full of milk in one hand and most of a kipper in the other. She had decided it would be fun to hide under a costume basket but nobody had come looking for her, and she was bored. The little girl sat down on the top step. Her legs were short, the steps were steep, and her hands were full of what was left of her supper. She decided it would be easiest to sit down and bump from one step to the next, so she did just that, then padded in bare feet across the grass to the lion.

Drina had half heard the lion's name when her father was talking earlier. It was something like "Sampots". When she tried to say it, it came out as "Jampot". The lion looked up all the same. She knelt in front of him, not noticing that his mane was matted with dirt and his face thin with hunger. She looked into his eyes, which were golden like amber and desperately sad.

Seeing at once that he was too big to drink from the little mug, she poured milk into her hand and let him lap it up. Her hand was very small so she had to keep filling it and a lot of milk ended up on the ground. The lion seemed to like it and kept on licking long after the milk was gone.

She offered him the kipper next, and smiled to hear him slurp it about on his tongue and crunch it with his few remaining teeth.

When he had finished eating, the lion licked his lips. Then he opened his red mouth very wide. Little Drina covered her face with her hands, not because she was afraid, but because his breath smelt so bad.

 3

Even when his bony jaws closed round her, she still wasn't afraid.

Like a mother cat with her kitten, the lion drew her close and laid her softly against his foreleg. That was where they found her a few minutes later, sleeping contentedly against the lion's mane.

# Chapter Two

Ten years later Drina Snapdragon sat on a rock by a wide blue-grey lake, swishing her feet in the water. She had one arm round Jampot, and her thick ginger hair and his long tawny mane blended together. The water made shushing noises and tickled her toes.

Twidings-on-Lullwater was Drina's favourite place in the world. This year, for the first time in her life, she could stay at Twidings for as long as she liked – or, at least, as long as Granny Annie needed her more than Snapdragon Family Circus did. She and Jampot would be here all summer.

She was enjoying herself so much by the lake that she didn't get that uneasy feeling – you know – the feeling that means somebody is watching you.

At the end of the lake was the shore with its silvery

white sand, and a low stone wall that wrapped around it like a protecting arm. Little trailing green plants spindled down from the wall, and on the other side was a narrow, bumpy road. It was from here that a tall, slim man watched Drina. He had very short, dark hair, thin on the top and turning grey at the edges, and a moustache like a little grey bottlebrush. He wore a suit; a pale grey one. He had been there for some time when Mrs Baggotty from the village shop came past.

"Who's that?" he asked her. "That girl with the lion?"

Mrs Baggotty, who was a short, neat person, put her hand on her hip and looked him up and down. Her way of thinking was that a conversation should begin with, "Good evening, Mrs Baggotty," or "How are you, Mrs Baggotty?" not "Who's that?" But the man didn't seem to see it that way.

"That's Annie Snapdragon's granddaughter," she said.

The man scowled. "Another one?"

"This one doesn't live here," explained Mrs Baggotty. "She's Elizabeth Andrina, same as her grandmother, but they call her Drina."

"Tell me more," he ordered.

Mrs Baggotty swallowed nervously. The man had that effect on people. "Her father's Freddie Snapdragon. He left the village to work in a circus," she said. "Now he has his own circus and three daughters. Drina's the youngest."

"What's she doing here?" the man demanded, but Mrs Baggotty was already scuttling away.

6

He asked himself the question instead. Mrs Snapdragon already had a bunch of grandchildren living in the village – the Fiddlestep family, who did tailoring and dressmaking – and he didn't like any of them. What was this new one doing here?

To know that, you would have to understand what had happened the night before, at Snapdragon Family Circus. . .

In the light of the setting sun, the Big Top glowed bright and golden like a pavilion in a medieval tournament. Inside was a warm smell of people and sawdust and excitement as all the performers gathered for the final swooping, soaring, terrifying finale. The fire-jugglers, called "The Family of Flames", stood on a platform and flung blazing torches into the air. They ran off as Amazonia the Strongest Woman in the World picked up the two Harlequin Clowns and carried them round the ring. Ma Snapdragon's little curly white dog, Pompom, ran round his obstacle course. The two older Snapdragon sisters, Sapphire and Spangle, somersaulted down from their trapezes and rode glossy black horses round the ring while Magnificent Merlin the Escapologist wriggled out from a locked and chained cage. As Sapphire and Spangle leapt down from their horses and bowed, the crowd rose to their feet and cheered.

Drina and the lion were sitting on a straw bale by the tent flap.

"Nearly time," said Drina. "Shall we put your teeth in? Yawn for Drina. Good lion."

She couldn't help pulling a face. Close up, Jampot's breath still smelt terrible.

The Snapdragons' only performing animals were Pompom and the two horses, who were all born show-offs and very well cared for. Jampot couldn't roar and hadn't many of his teeth left, so as soon as she was old enough Drina had made him a set of false ones, which he wore when he needed to look majestic. She was good at making things, and understood that teeth gave him dignity. They looked just like the real thing, but he didn't wear them much because he couldn't eat with them in. However, he always joined in for the final parade around the circus ring and he wore his teeth for that.

Drina rubbed lion spit off her fingers.

"Good boy," she said. "Are you ready? March!"

They stepped out proudly, side by side, following the band and the horses. Drina had to wave to the crowd and watch where she put her feet at the same time. At last Pa Snapdragon led them out of the tent and into the summer evening, and the circus was over. The Family of Flames lit the way for the crowd as they trailed out of the Big Top towards home.

"All done now, Jampot," said Drina. "Good lion." She stroked his deep, thick mane and he plodded beside her to his wagon, which was really a very large cage on wheels. Drina had made curtains to protect his privacy and kept it spotlessly clean, with fresh straw every day and blankets in winter. When she had taken out his teeth, ("May I have your teeth, please, Jampot? Thank

you") and given him his porridge, it was time h
her favourite things, which was grooming him.

She chose a brush and combed his long, gold
so that loose hairs floated into the air. Very gently
smoothed the tangles from his mane and sponged his
paws with cool water. He almost purred and Drina
leaned her face against him, loving the feel and the
smell of her big, solid, contented lion. Then she sat
back and looked into his dark amber eyes.

"Happy?" she asked. She discussed everything with
Jampot. It was as if they shared each other's thoughts.

Pa said that Drina always had good ideas. She was
the best at solving problems and knowing what to do
in an emergency. Drina felt that her ideas came from
Jampot. He helped her to be calm and to think deeply.
(Ma said Drina had too much imagination, which
meant that she was no good at flying from trapezes
or riding galloping horses while doing handstands,
because she could always imagine what might happen
if she fell off.)

Jampot had grown up in a circus where he didn't
belong. Drina sometimes felt that she didn't know what
she was doing in a circus, either.

Drina stayed with Jampot until he rolled on to his
side and began, very softly, to snore, then she drew the
curtains and tiptoed back to the overcrowded wagon
that she shared with her parents and sisters.

Amazonia the Strongest Woman in the World was
passing by. "You want to look out, love," she said.
"There's an almighty row going on in your wagon."

9

Drina liked Amazonia. Her muscles were so bulky and knotted that normal clothes wouldn't fit over them and everything she wore had to be specially made. Drina had knitted her a sweater from Granny's homespun wool, and knew that Amazonia treasured it. One day when Jampot had cut his paw, Amazonia had picked him up very gently, carried him to Drina, and helped her to dress the wound. She was one of the kindest people Drina knew.

"Thanks for the warning," said Drina, and climbed up the steps.

The outside of the Snapdragon wagon was painted red and gold and looked as bright and cheerful as a toyshop window. Inside it was too small and smelt of damp washing and fried bacon. Costumes hung from rails on the ceiling, spilled out of baskets and lay in a huge pile on the clothes horse. The frying smell came from the back of the wagon where Pa was making bacon sandwiches. Sapphire and Spangle were wearing their red dressing gowns. They still had their circus make-up on and their hair was tied back so tightly that Drina wondered how they could shut their eyes. They were quarrelling, which happened a lot. Drina sat down on a pile of velvet cloaks and suddenly her sisters stopped arguing and looked at her.

"Drina can go!" they both said.

"Where?" asked Drina.

Spangle turned to Sapphire. "But then there'd be nobody to look after the costumes," she said.

"Go where?" repeated Drina.

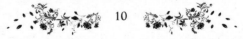

Sapphire sighed. "And she's too young."

Drina stood up. "Excuse me!" she said. "Where do you want me to go?"

Pa appeared from behind the stove with a plate of bacon sandwiches. He offered them to Drina first. "You weren't here when we got the message, love," he said. "When we got back after the show there was a letter for us. Your Granny Annie's had a fall."

"Is she all right?" asked Drina. She loved Granny Annie as much as she loved Jampot.

"She will be," said Pa. "But she's broken her arm and she could do with somebody with her for a while, to help her. It's difficult to spare anyone from the circus."

"I don't see why any of us should go," remarked Spangle. "She's got Aunt Jemima and Uncle Tam and all the Fiddlestep cousins already."

"I'm sure the Fiddlesteps are doing all they can," said Pa. "But they're very busy and work extremely hard, and my mother needs someone to stay with her."

"We can't spare Drina!" said Ma. "She may be no good at acrobatics, but give the girl her due, she works wonders sewing the costumes. And who'd look after the lion?"

"He could come with me," said Drina. "Granny won't mind."

Ma put down her mug of tea so she could put both hands on her hips and look grumpy and sensible at the same time.

"And how are we supposed to go about this?" she demanded. "We're fifteen miles from Twidings and heading in the opposite direction. We can't trail the whole circus there to drop Drina off."

"I'll take Drina as far as Carillon in the morning," said Pa. "And from there she can catch the Day Train if it's running."

"I'll walk down from Carillon," said Drina quickly. "I don't need the Day Train."

The Day Train had been invented by Nithering Day, a Twidings man. Whenever they could get it to work it lurched, rocked and roared from the town of Carillon through a string of hillside villages to Twidings-on-Lullwater. It only ran on the days when there was somebody to drive it, and only if it was all in one piece. Drina's imagination was the reason she didn't trust the Day Train. She could see in her mind what would happen if it didn't stop before it got to the lake.

Drina worked out that if she and Jampot reached Carillon by midday they could be in Twidings by evening. Jampot was getting old and slow, but it was downhill all the way. It was midsummer, so they would get there in daylight.

"What are you smiling about?" asked Spangle suspiciously.

"Nothing," she said.

She wasn't going to tell anyone but Jampot.

The next day, walking down through the hills to Twidings, Drina said, "Tell you what I think, Jampot. When we were talking about who should go to Twidings, Spangle said that the Fiddlesteps could look

12

after Granny. Well, they could, and I'm sure they do. But I think Granny knew that I wanted to be there, and that if she asked for somebody to go, it would be me – I mean, us. It's by the lake, and the lake is full of fish, and you love fish – oh, look!"

The village of Twidings-on-Lullwater appeared before them, the wall curling round the lake and the cottages dotted about in clusters. Boats bobbed on the water. Sunlight on the lake sparkled so brightly that she had to shade her eyes.

Granny Annie's cottage looked as if it had grown there. The little wooden gate squeaked a welcome and in the cottage garden pinks, lavender, rosemary, white bee balm, purple foxgloves and many-coloured snapdragons tumbled over each other and spilled on to the path. The house was built of honey-coloured stone but in summer, what with honeysuckles, roses and hollyhocks growing up and strawberries in hanging baskets growing down, you could hardly see anything but the windows.

Drina knocked, but there was no answer.

The back door was locked too. Granny was often in the garden where she grew fruit, flowers and vegetables, and hung out her washing, but she wasn't there this evening.

"She didn't know we'd come today," said Drina to Jampot. "We'll go to the lake."

She picked some strawberries, knowing that Granny wouldn't mind, and shared them with Jampot as they walked down to Lullwater Lake, which was as wide

as the village and a hundred times as long – or almost. They drank from the fresh cold spring, then sat on the rock where Drina pulled off her shoes and socks and splashed her feet in the water. The rock was warm with sunshine and Jampot sat beside her, watching the fish as all cats do.

"How long do you think a broken arm takes to mend?" she asked him. "I want Granny to be well, but I hope she needs me for ages. And we'll see Billy and Taffeta again."

Billy and Taffeta Fiddlestep were Drina's favourite cousins. Billy was about her own age and Taffeta a little younger. *Jampot, Granny Annie, Billy, Taffeta, the lake.* Life was as good as it could possibly be.

Under her hand, she felt Jampot's muscles stiffen.

"What's the matter?" she said. "It's quite safe, we're in Twidings."

He stood, growled softly and placed himself in front of Drina as he did when he wanted to protect her. But when Drina turned round she saw only a man in a pale grey suit walking away towards the Village Green.

# Chapter Three

"It's Drina! Look, Granny, it's Drina and Jampot!"

Drina turned and jumped to her feet. Taffeta Fiddlestep, bright and colourful in her patchwork dress, was leaping across the shore to meet her. She hurled herself so hard into Drina's arms that they both fell over, then she threw her arms round Jampot and rubbed her face in his mane. Taffeta's wild dark curls often had bits of leaf and twig caught in them, and by the time she let go of Jampot there were tufts of lion fur in there as well. Lion hair clung to her gold-and-purple jacket. Drina picked herself up, then her shoes, and climbed the wall to where Granny Annie stood smiling.

Jampot relaxed. The man he didn't like had gone away. He liked Taffeta and Granny Annie. There might be fish for tea.

Even with her arm in plaster and a sling, Granny Annie looked as neat and pretty as a snowdrop. She was hardly any taller than Drina, with delicate bones and silver white hair, and as usual she was dressed in the old-fashioned Twider style: full skirt, bodice and lacy white blouse. Twined into her hair were two hairpins decorated with blue butterflies that looked so real that they might have flown away. Drina knew that Granny Annie had made them herself. She hugged her grandmother gently, afraid of hurting her.

"My Drina!" said Granny Annie, and as she smiled her face creased like tissue paper, her eyes twinkled, and she was even more beautiful. "How sweet of you to come! And the lion too! How lovely! I've just been to see Dr Janet, and then I met Taffeta on the way home and we saw you sitting so peacefully there with Jampot. It will be so nice to have a lion around the house. What does he eat?"

"Anything soft," said Drina. "He loves fish."

"We've got lots of that," said Taffeta. She clambered on to the wall and walked along, balancing with her arms like a tightrope-walker. Drina often thought that Taffeta should be the one in the circus. She even looked the part. Her jacket was too big for her and her dress was made up of scraps of lace and satin in different shades of blue, purple and gold. That was what came of being youngest child of a tailor and a dressmaker.

Taffeta jumped down from the wall. "Where did Gerbil go?" she asked.

16

"What gerbil?" asked Drina.

"Not *a* gerbil. *Gerbil*," said Taffeta. "Gerbil Cravat. Gerbil like the animal, cravat like a posh sort of necktie. He was watching you just now."

"He's new to the village, Drina, dear," explained Granny Annie. "A quiet person. He keeps to himself. He doesn't fish or row a boat or any such thing, so I don't suppose he'll stay here much longer."

"His hair sticks up like a brush. You can see the top of his head through it," said Taffeta. "And he's got a little moustache like a fuzzy grey caterpillar. It looks as if it crawled down his nose."

"Taffeta!" said Granny, but she didn't seem cross.

They had reached her cottage by now. Granny Annie gave Drina the key. The door swung open to the smell of wool, roses and smoked fish.

One long room stretched from the front of the cottage to the back. At the back was the kitchen with a stove, a worktop and a sink, a clothes horse and two plain chairs. At the other end Granny Annie's rocking chair sat in the bay window. The sun made bright patches on the floor and reflected off the spines of books in the bookshelf, which had faded in the light. Drina looked with longing at that bookshelf. (There wasn't much room for books in a circus wagon.) There were a dining table and chairs on one side of the room and on the other was a fireplace, with two more saggy, comfortable old chairs and a low stool, Granny's spinning wheel, and a basket of fleece. Usually the dining table would also used for Granny's sewing, but

 17

now that her arm was in plaster there were no materials laid out.

Jampot walked thoughtfully about in front of the fireplace. In winter there would be a crackling blaze leaping up the chimney, but in summer the grate was cool and filled with flowers and fir cones. The best place to enjoy the warmth was in front of the sunny window. He rolled over and sighed happily. This was heaven.

On the other side of the front door was a small parlour where Granny kept her best china, a huge wooden chest full of old letters, and odds and ends of wool and fabric. Behind the parlour was the wash house, with a tub, a stick for pounding the washing and a boiler to heat the water. It was also the bathroom. When Drina and Taffeta had been small, Granny used to bath them side by side in the washtub.

"Mum brought some supper round, but we have to cook it," announced Taffeta.

Drina cooked the fish while Taffeta cut oddly shaped chunks of fresh brown bread and slathered them with butter, sucking her finger where she'd cut it ("Just a teeny cut, Granny"). Granny picked strawberries and poured cream over them.

By the time everybody (including Jampot) had eaten and everyone (except Jampot) had curled up in armchairs for a chat, Drina was realizing what a long day she'd had. She was thinking about bed.

"We can go reeding tomorrow, if you like," said Taffeta. She wriggled down from her chair and settled on the floor beside Jampot.

"I'm here to look after Granny," answered Drina.

"Oh, you go with Taffeta," said Granny. "If you just help me get dressed and do the breakfast, that'll be me sorted out. Those reeds need to be done."

"Good," decided Taffeta. "I'll call in the morning, and we can go and get Billy. He doesn't live at home any more. He lives in a tree."

"A tree!?" said Drina.

"You know what a squash it is in our house," explained Taffeta. "There's still only ten of us but the older ones take up more and more space. In fact Satin wants to build another house next door... Anyway, Billy made a treehouse in the wood. He only comes home when he feels like it."

Drina yawned and Taffeta giggled.

"Dopey Drina," she said.

"Drina, what time were you up this morning?" asked Granny.

"Sixish, I think," said Drina.

Taffeta gasped. "That's before thud!" she said, but before Drina could ask what thud was, Granny was bustling her up the stairs to bed.

From the landing there were two bedrooms, Granny's on one side and a little spare bedroom on the other, next to a stair leading to the attic. Drina helped Granny with her hair, her nightie and her sling, picked up some hairpins from the floor and kissed her goodnight.

At the door of her own little room, she gasped with delight. The bed by the window was covered in one of

Granny's patchwork quilts, mostly in blue and yellow, with a spare blanket folded at the foot. There was a chest of drawers with a large flowery jug and basin for hot water, an empty fireplace, and a rag rug on the white painted floorboards. Framing the windows were curtains of deep blue decorated with silver stars. She had forgotten how lovely it all was.

Gently she touched the quilt, the soft plump pillow and the china jug. She ran her fingers down the curtains, then opened the window and leaned out. Over the lake, the light was fading. Swans floated on the water. The waves shushed on the shore. She spread out her arms and revolved slowly, because she could. Last night she had slept in the tiny bottom bunk in the wagon with Spangle in the bed above her and a costume basket at her head. Tonight she didn't have to share with anyone except Jampot. Steadily, happily, she brushed him down and spread the spare blanket on the floor for him.

It was too good for sleep, too good even for reading in bed. She wanted to lie awake feeling the freshness of the sheets, listening to the lake, trailing her arm out of the bed so she could stroke Jampot's curling mane, breathing in the fresh clear air.

Jampot sniffed round the room and decided that Drina would be safe here. He had walked a long way and was tired. He licked Drina's hand and fell asleep. Jampot never asked for much. He had Drina.

*

Taffeta was on the doorstep before Drina was out of bed.

"It's too early," yawned Drina, clambering down the stairs and opening the door.

"Is it?" said Taffeta. "The birds have been chirping about for hours. I couldn't sleep. Is Granny up?"

Gooseberries and cream seemed a funny thing to have for breakfast, but the bushes in the garden were full of berries and they needed using up. When Granny was dressed and breakfast cleared away, Taffeta led the way into the wood on the west side of the village. They went left, right and up a hill until they stood beneath a tall, spreading oak tree with a wooden ladder against it.

Taffeta tucked her too-long skirt into her knickers and began to climb. "Can lions climb trees?" she asked.

"Oh yes," said Drina. "But I don't know what would happen when he got to the top." The platform above them looked rickety and lopsided. "Jampot, stay."

Jampot lay down contentedly and cleaned his paws, and Drina followed Taffeta up the ladder. They stopped when they reached a bridge of planks, which led to a small shelter built from branches and more planks, with a bit of tarpaulin over the top. It was shaped rather like a bird house or cuckoo clock, but much bigger and it had a curtain where a real house would have a door. Through a gap in the curtain they could see a sort of stove on metal legs, washstand made of a few sticks, and two bottles of water. A candlehat – a white hat with

 21

a broad brim and candles set into it, for going out in the dark – hung on a peg on the roof.

"Follow me exactly," whispered Taffeta. She tiptoed from plank to plank, with Drina following cautiously, and drew back the curtain without a sound.

The treehouse had one window, a proper glass one, half open. Opposite it was a groundsheet and a nest of pillows and blankets. Drina could see Billy's curly brown head sticking out. Taffeta pointed to the window.

On the sill lay the biggest sparrow Drina had ever seen. It lay on its back with its claws in the air and Drina would have thought it was dead except for the rise and fall of its chest and a gentle twittering snore. As she watched, it began, very slowly, to roll over. She reached forward, but Taffeta put a hand on her arm to stop her.

"It's all right," whispered Taffeta. "You'll see!"

The sparrow rolled steadily until it was on the very edge of the sill, tipped over, hit the floor with a thud and opened one eye, with a tweet that sounded more like "ouch". Billy poked his head out from the covers, grunted at Taffeta and sat up.

"Hello, Drina!" he said.

But Drina was kneeling beside the sparrow, looking anxious.

"He's fine, he's gone back to sleep," said Taffeta. She pulled the covers off her brother and sat on the floor beside Drina. "He does this every day, that's why he's called Thud. He's Billy's alarm clock."

"Doesn't he get hurt?" asked Drina.

22

"Who, our Billy? Oh, the sparrow... No, he can still fly, even though he's too big for his wings and he has to take a run at it. Billy, you've been sleeping in your clothes again."

"Just as well, isn't it, with you here," said Billy. He shook out his blankets, pushed his fingers through his hair, dabbled his hands in the water and rubbed them on his trousers. Then he started to eat an apple.

"We're going reeding," said Taffeta. "Do you want to come?"

"Sure," he said, and turned to Drina with a big grin across his wide mouth. "What blew you in?"

Even in term time there were days when Twider children didn't go to school but instead helped with farming, fishing and twiding. Twiding was what the village was famous for. Tall, silvery green reeds grew around the lake, quite different from the reeds anywhere else in the world, and they grew as fast as you picked them. They smelt like freshly cut grass and it was amazing what you could do with them. The villagers made a kind of fine, soft rope from them called twide, and you could make twide into all sorts of things – baskets, fishing nets, mats, paper, and a sort of material that looked like sacking but wasn't so scratchy. Twide gave the village its name.

Sheds around the lakeside were used for storing the twide, and others for dyeing it and soaking it and walking all over it to make it squishy, depending on what you wanted to use it for. The sheds were called

"mecessaries" because to prepare twide it was necessary to make a mess. Granny Annie said that Drina, being so good with her hands, was a born twider.

Drina, Billy and Taffeta chatted on the way to the shore, catching up with each other's news and their plans for the summer and whether Mr Day had blown anything up this week. Jampot raised his head and his nostrils widened. Somewhere in the air was such a delicious whiff of lake water that he felt younger already, and he licked Drina's hand to thank her for bringing him here.

When they waded out to pull the tall smooth reeds from the water's edge, Jampot stepped slowly, paw by paw, into the lake.

"Go on then," said Drina, watching. "Look, Taffeta, he's loving this!"

Jampot walked on steadily. When the water was up to his shoulders and his mane was spreading and floating on the top, he ducked his head and swam. Watching him, Drina had almost forgot that she was supposed to be reeding.

Taffeta interrupted her thoughts. "Billy, Gerbil Cravat was watching Drina last night." She struggled with some reeds that were taller than she was. She turned to Drina. "I don't like him. He makes me feel squirmy."

Drina remembered how Jampot had growled at the stranger. "Does anybody know why Mr Cravat came here?"

"Nobody has a clue." Billy shook water from a bunch

24

of reeds and spread them on the white sand of the shore. "He's secretive. Granny thought he wouldn't stay long. But he's ordered some clothes from Mum and Dad, so he might be planning to stay a while."

"What sort of clothes?" asked Drina.

"Don't know," said Billy.

"I could find out," offered Taffeta. She left the reeds and began to do handstands, which she couldn't quite manage. "Tell you what, though. . ." She turned the right way up and shook sand out of her hair. "We've had tons and tons of black velvet delivered, and Satin says they've ordered satin too. That might be for him."

All the Fiddlestep children were named after fabrics, except Billy. By the time Billy was born they couldn't think of any more fabric names for a boy, so they said, "Billy will do", and he was always Billy Will-Do after that.

"What does he want velvet and satin for?" asked Billy. "He always wears a suit. Everyone else round here keeps suits for best. Even Squire Thumping-Jolly goes around in a shabby old tweed jacket and patched trousers."

Taffeta rolled over laughing in the sand. "Gerbil in black velvet!" she said.

Jampot swam to the shore and shook himself dry. "Hello, you!" said Taffeta, sitting up.

But Jampot was looking past her at something.

"Jampot, what have you seen?" asked Drina. "Oh, it's Poodle!"

"Look out, here he comes!" cried Taffeta.

Hurtling downhill towards them was a blur of dog, moulting grey hairs as it went. It was the size of a wolf, with extremely long limbs and no control over them.

"He always looked as if he has too many legs," observed Drina. "And they don't all stop at the same time. Or in the same place. Poodle! Here!"

They all watched to see which bit of Poodle would stop first.

On seeing Jampot the front of Poodle stopped so sharply that the back end of Poodle was surprised and fell over it. He stepped backwards and put his tail between his hind legs as soon as he'd worked out where they were.

"Don't be silly, Poodle, you know Jampot," said Drina.

Jampot and Poodle sniffed round each other and remembered that they were old friends. Poodle knew that Jampot hadn't much energy but was calm, strong and, more to the point, a lion, and deserved respect, so he rolled over.

Poodle belonged to the Thumping-Jolly family who lived at Thumping Old Hall. Drina shaded her eyes to see which of the family was following him. The Squire in his old tweeds? The Honourable Mrs Veronica Thumping-Jolly, who always wore pearls at one end and wellies at the other? It couldn't be their son Tarquin; he was at college in Carillon – no, it was their daughter Daffodil who appeared, breathless from running. She was a little older and taller than Drina and Billy.

She had thick blonde hair in plaits and talked a lot, and loudly.

"Hello, Drina!" she called. "Hello, lion!"

Jampot settled at Drina's feet, glad that he belonged to her and not to Daffodil.

"His name's Jampot," Drina reminded her, and hugged Poodle. Poodle wasn't intelligent, but he was very affectionate. His name was unfortunate: when he was a puppy and Daffodil was a little girl, she had insisted that he was a poodle, so everybody called him that. Daffodil herself was named after the first thing her mother saw when she looked out of the window after her birth. Squire Thumping-Jolly said she should really have been called "Gardener Boot Wheeling a Barrow-load of Manure to the Rhubarb Patch", but they chose Daffodil instead.

"I thought I'd find you two Fiddlesteps down here," said Daffodil loudly, flopping on to the sand. "Listen to this! Gerbil Cravat came to the Hall this morning."

"Lucky you," said Billy.

"That's not the exciting bit," said Daffodil. "He wants to buy the castle!"

Taffeta shrieked with laughter. "It's falling down!" she said.

"What does he want it for?" asked Billy.

"Just to be grand, I should think," said Daffodil. "So he can say he's King of the Castle. He might want to rebuild it."

"I like it the way it is," said Taffeta.

"And we won't be able to go there any more," Drina

told her. "Not if he rebuilds it. Your family shared it with everyone."

"Then he *does* mean to stay," said Billy, frowning as he shook the reeds dry. "If he's buying the castle, he must want to live here."

"I suppose it's all right," said Taffeta. "If you can live in a tree, he can live in a castle. He can go round it dressed up in black velvet!" She rolled over in the sand, laughing again.

Jampot gave a gentle growl, not his warning growl but the happy one, like a purr, that he used to greet people he liked.

Granny Annie was pattering down to meet them with a basket on her good arm.

Drina ran to meet her. "Granny, let me carry that," she said. "I shouldn't have left you for so long."

"Nonsense, dear, I'm managing perfectly well," she said. "I thought you'd be ready for some elderflower fizz and biscuits. And here's Daffodil and Poodle too. What a good thing I brought plenty."

They sat in the sun and Drina dunked biscuits in elderflower fizz to make them soft for Jampot, but when they told Granny about Gerbil buying the castle, Granny stopped with a biscuit halfway to her mouth. She put it down and stared in front of her. She turned her head to the left then to the front again, and pursed up her lips as if she'd just bitten a lemon. Granny always did this when she was concentrating or trying to remember something.

"He mustn't!" said Granny at last. "He mustn't buy it! Go and stop him!"

"Why, Granny?" asked Drina.

"Because whoever owns the castle owns the village!" cried Granny. "The shore, the lake, everything!"

"I didn't know that!" said Daffodil.

"I don't suppose your parents did either!" said Granny. "But I'm sure Gerbil Cravat does! Run to the Hall and tell them!"

# Chapter Four

The way to Thumping Old Hall led up a track that grew rougher, stonier and steeper all the way, and Drina had a painful stitch in her side by the time they reached the top. She had left Jampot with Granny, but Poodle bounded along beside her, so the sheep in the fields bleated with disapproval, and chickens scratching about outside the Hall scattered in a flurry of feathers.

The Hall was a long, weather-worn building made from stone at the old end and red bricks at the new end. They ran under the wide archway to the courtyard and Daffodil peered in at a window.

"They're not in the parlour," she called, and ran to the next one, "or the dining room either. They must be in Daddy's study!"

"Is that bad?" asked Billy.

"It's where he signs things!" she wailed.

The dark oak door of the Hall was unlocked. Daffodil bolted upstairs with the rest of them following and they all tumbled into Squire Thumping-Jolly's study where shelves crammed with books reached to the ceiling, and tall cabinets were so full of papers that the drawers wouldn't shut properly. On the big, gleaming table in the middle of the room was a neatly written document. Poodle fell over Taffeta as they came to a halt.

Squire Thumping-Jolly stood there, round-faced and smiling in his old tweed suit. Beside him was Daffodil's mum, the Honourable Veronica Thumping-Jolly, looking elegant in a simple dress and pearls and wellies. Their housekeeper, Mrs Pinn, was there in her neat black gown, and so was Dennis Boot the gardener. At one end of the table stood Gerbil Cravat in his pale grey suit, with his head tilted up a little as if he were afraid of his moustache falling off. He was tucking a pen into his inside pocket.

"No!" yelled Daffodil. The Squire winced.

"Daffodil!" said the Honourable Veronica. "Children!"

"Dad!" said Daffodil, getting her breath back, "You mustn't sell the castle!"

"It's a bit late for that, Daffy," said the Squire, also putting away a pen. "You mustn't mind. We don't need the castle, and Mr Cravat has plans for it."

Drina and Billy wriggled past to look down at the paper on the table. Everything was completed and signed – *Veronica Florence Thumping-Jolly (Hon),*

31

*Squire Romulus Jason Thumping-Jolly* (*Colonel, retired*) and, in a very small, neat hand, *G. Cravat*. Dennis and Mrs Pinn had signed as witnesses.

Gerbil and the Squire were shaking hands.

"It's a pleasure to do business with you, Colonel," said Gerbil. It was the first time Drina had heard him speak and his voice was light and thin, as if he were whining about something. "I shall very much enjoy owning Twidings village and your delightful lake."

"Owning?" repeated the Squire. "I don't think I understand you, Mr Cravat."

"I'm sure that's not right," said the Honourable Veronica.

"Ah, but it is, madam," said Gerbil. He reached into his inside pocket again and drew out a thin book with a faded red cover. "You'll find it all in here. The Ancient Laws regarding the Lordship of the village of Twidings and the Lake known as Lullwater. You can check with the Government Office at Carillon if you like. It's the real thing, I assure you. I have the right to be known as the Lord of Lullwater."

"Nonsense!" exclaimed the Honourable Veronica.

"I've never been Lord of Lullwater!" protested the Squire.

"Oh, but you were, while you owned the castle," said Gerbil. "You just didn't know it. You should have taken more care."

"Well, you're certainly not Lord of Thumping Old Hall!" said the Squire.

"Indeed," said Gerbil, still in that whining voice.

 32

"The Old Hall is not part of my territory. There are limits to the rights of the Lord of Lullwater." He gave a sudden smile like a crocodile showing its teeth. "Limits, but not very many. I will be moving into the castle by the end of the week." He turned and glared down at Taffeta, with his head a little on one side like a bird observing a worm. "You're one of those Fiddlestep girls, aren't you? Tell your parents to have my new clothes delivered there by Friday."

Taffeta gazed steadily back at him. "I'll *ask* them," she said. "I can't *tell* my parents things. I mean, I can tell them whether I'm happy or not or whether we've had a good reeding day. But I can't tell them what to do."

"Shut up, Taffy," said Daffodil miserably. Her parents seemed too stunned to say anything at all. "You'll only make it worse."

"Worse?" repeated Gerbil, still with his crocodile smile. "I don't know what you mean. I'm sure we'll all get along very well. Twidings is about to become a most exciting place." He pushed past them and ran briskly down the stairs.

"What have we done?" gasped Mrs Thumping-Jolly, clutching her pearls so tightly Drina thought they'd snap.

"And what's *he* going to do?" wondered Drina, wishing she had Jampot beside her.

"He might not do much," said Daffodil hopefully. "He might just dress up like a lord and live in the castle. He'll have to put a roof on it. And rebuild

33

the falling-down bits. And put in furniture and kitchen stuff and everything and taps and a—"

"He said it was going to get *exciting*," said Taffeta. "I like exciting, but I don't think I'll like his sort of exciting."

"Do you suppose that book was genuine?" asked Daffodil. "He might have just made it out of something and it doesn't really prove that he's the Lord of Lullwater."

"But it's true anyway," said Billy. "Even if that book is a fake he's right about owning the castle and everything, because Granny Annie knew about it. And now we have to tell her that we didn't get here in time to stop him."

Drina slipped an arm round Taffeta, who looked ready to cry. "Who's going to tell Granny?" she asked.

"We'll all tell her," said Drina.

They told her at lunchtime, as they sat at the table. Taffeta didn't eat much. Jampot knew Drina was upset and leaned against her to comfort her, as he always did.

"We should have run faster," said Taffeta. "We were nearly in time."

"You did your best," said Granny kindly. "And this village has put up with all sorts of trouble over the years. I've seen those sudden lake storms when the water churned up and surged so far through the village that you could catch a fish without leaving your own front door. We all survived and got back to normal."

"But when that happens you usually get a feeling

about it, Granny, and you can warn us," said Taffeta. "Nobody knew that Gerbil was going to take over the village."

Jampot left Drina briefly to lean against Taffeta.

"Perhaps it should have occurred to me that he might," said Granny.

"Granny, how did you know?" asked Drina. "How did you know that whoever owned the castle owns the village?"

"The Lullwater Laws," said Granny. "My father and his father knew about them. They had a little book of them, probably like the one that Mr Cravat had. Nobody ever bothered about them much because Twidings normally runs itself perfectly well without any laws. We still have the Quarter Courts every three months, when the judge comes from Carillon to sort out any problems, but there's never much for her to do. There are two policemen in Carillon but it takes a long time for them to get here. We sort ourselves out."

"What happened to your father's book of the laws?" asked Drina.

"It's too late for that," said Billy.

Drina called Jampot to her to help her think. "It's not too late," she said. "We need a copy of *The Lullwater Laws*. If we can find a law that Gerbil breaks, we can report him to the judge at the next Quarter Court. There might be laws that he doesn't want us to know about."

"Court will be in two months' time," said Granny. "Now, let me think." She did her concentrating and

sucking-a-lemon face again. "What happened to that book? I believe my father gave it away, and I can't remember who to. But there's something in there about the duties of the Lord of Lullwater."

"Ooh, what are they?" said Taffeta, suddenly looking happier.

Granny smiled and her eyes twinkled. "I can remember one of them," she said. "The Lord of Lullwater must be married to a woman from the village."

"Got him!" shouted Billy.

"But," went on Granny, and Taffeta's face fell again, "if he's a single man he must marry a Twidings girl within twenty-eight days of becoming Lord."

"Then we have to stop him from marrying anyone local," decided Drina.

"That's all right, then," said Taffeta. "Who'd marry him?"

Billy sighed. "Somebody who wants a castle," he said. "And he'll be so desperate to get married, he'll try his hardest."

"Billy's right," said Drina, stroking Jampot thoughtfully. "We need to warn all the single women. He'll be running after them..."

"...and giving them great big buckets of flowers," said Taffeta.

"It's 'bouquets', Taff," said Billy.

"And saying, 'Oh, you are so beautiful!'" went on Taffeta. She knelt in front of Jampot and gazed into his eyes. "He'll be saying, 'You are so beautiful, you have

beautiful eyes and beautiful ears and beautiful noses, will you marry me?'"

"Think," said Drina firmly. "Who will he ask?"

Billy sat bolt upright. "My big sisters!" he said.

By two o'clock that day everybody in Twidings knew that Gerbil Cravat was now the Lord of Lullwater. This was partly because Daffodil Thumping-Jolly went down to the village and told everyone she met, and then knocked on all the cottage doors to tell everyone she hadn't met. Also, Gerbil had written out a notice and tied it to the tree on the Village Green. It read:

*I, Gerbil Fundamental Cravat, solemnly declare that, on this twentieth day of June, I purchased the Castle of Twidings-on-Lullwater and am therefore the owner of Lullwater Lake and its shores and all the land within four hundred yards of the shore, and will be known from now on henceforth and for ever as Gerbil, Lord of Lullwater.*

By three o'clock, three gerbils, four funny faces and a cat had been drawn on the notice. By five, Billy and Drina had talked to all the single young women in the village, starting with Billy's sisters, Velvet, Satin and Linen, and working their way round the doctor, the vicar's daughters, the dentist, Kate Applemint at the post office and the girls who worked in the mecessaries.

They were only just in time. By nightfall Gerbil had

 37

already asked Velvet Fiddlestep to marry him. He'd also proposed to Kate Applemint and the Butterscotch twins. Granny said she was most put out because he hadn't asked her.

Drina went to bed thinking of the book of *The Lullwater Laws* and where to find a copy. Jampot knew that she was puzzling about something but didn't know how to help, which was frustrating. He had more energy since he came to Twidings and wanted to use it.

In the morning Drina, Taffeta and Jampot were at Billy's tree at thud. Billy had climbed high into the tree and was craning his neck to get a good view of something.

"Get up here!" he called. "There's something happening at the castle!"

Drina had never cared for climbing rope ladders in the circus, but trees were all right. She and Taffeta scrambled high into the branches and looked out towards the castle.

At least ten horse-drawn wagons were there, and more were working their way down to the village. Men were unloading cartloads of wood, stone and bricks and carrying them to the ruins.

"He said he wanted to move in by the end of the week, and it's Wednesday," said Taffeta. "He's making it move-into-able. Shall we go and get a proper look?"

"Not me," said Billy. "I'm going fishing."

Drina and Taffeta heard clanging and hammering

before they were even near the castle. Jampot growled and Drina stroked his mane. Daffodil was there, chasing Poodle out of a tray of cement.

"He didn't do any harm," she said firmly. "He was just sniffing about, the way he does. He wanted to know what was going on. They were mixing cement and he didn't know what it was so he went to find out about it, didn't you, Poodle? And now it's very good cement because it's got Poodle's wee in it, and they should be pleased because that'll help to mix it up and make it strong and it'll be part of the castle for ever and ever. They're building up the walls and putting a roof on and then they're going to do a proper floor and everything."

A red-faced man was pushing a squeaky barrow full of bricks past them. Jampot placed himself between Drina and the squeaky thing.

"His Lordship wants it ready to move into by the weekend," said the man. "We'll have to work like smoke. Granted, it's a small castle as castles go, but all the same, cement takes time to set. If you know any big strong village lads who want a day's work send them along, we can use them." He caught sight of Jampot's back. "What an ogging big dog! What sort is he?"

"A lion," said Drina. "He won't hurt you."

The man looked at Jampot as if he'd like to believe it but couldn't, then wheeled his barrow quickly into the castle.

Taffeta turned to Drina. "What did he mean, 'ogging'?" she asked.

"They say it in Trabbershire," said Drina. "He talks with a Trabbershire accent too. It just means 'very', I suppose. We take the circus to Trabbershire and they say things like 'ogging good show' or 'it's ogging cold tonight'. I wonder why they're working here for Gerbil? They're a long way from home."

"Probably because he knew nobody round here would work for him," said Billy. "It was such a dirty trick taking over the village like that. None of the Twidings men would work for him, whatever he paid them."

"I don't know," said Drina thoughtfully, with her fingers in Jampot's mane. "I think they might."

"Look," said Taffeta. "More wagons! All that can't just be for the castle. What else is he building?"

"A prison?" said Billy. "Drina, what do you think?"

"Sorry?" said Drina. She was looking at Jampot and wondering whether the Twidings men would work for Gerbil.

"What do you think. . ." began Billy, then, "Look out, he's coming."

"Quiet, Jampot," said Drina. He was growling again. Gerbil Cravat came towards them wearing his usual pale grey suit, with his head tipped back a little.

"Billy Fiddlestep," he said in the whining voice that made Drina want to squirm. "How old is your sister Linen?"

"Dunno," answered Billy.

"Eighteen and she doesn't want to get married," said Taffeta promptly.

Gerbil glared at her then turned to Drina, his head on one side. "Miss Snapdragon," he said, "I do not like lions. Keep it under control, otherwise I will have to take serious action. And here comes your grandmother."

He strode back to the castle, snapping orders at the men who were putting up the scaffolding. The children turned and ran down to meet Granny.

"Are you all right, Granny?" asked Drina. "Do you want help with anything?"

"Not at all," said Granny brightly. "I only came to tell you I remembered what happened to our book of *The Lullwater Laws*. My father gave it to the Thumping-Jolly family because they'd lost theirs. It should still be at the Hall!"

"No, it isn't," announced Daffodil. "I would have seen it."

"But you haven't been looking for it!" said Taffeta. "Come on!"

She ran up towards the Hall with Poodle scampering after her. Billy and Daffodil followed.

"Off you go, Drina," said Granny. "Do you want to leave Jampot with me?"

"I'll take him," said Drina. "I need to think of something, and I think better with Jampot. Billy was saying that none of the local men would help to work on the castle. But I think they might – I mean, they sort of might, if..."

"Oh, I see!" said Granny. "Well, well. Yes, I think they might. Off you go with the others."

 41

"I've absolutely no idea," said Veronica Thumping-Jolly when they asked her about the book. "It must be in the library. That's where books go."

Drina stood in the library and turned round slowly, craning her neck so much that it hurt. She had never imagined that there could be so many books. It was as if this room were made of them. She wanted to run her fingers along the shelves until she found one that looked as if she might like it, then sit down against a warm Jampot and read.

"I'll climb up, you hold the ladder," said Taffeta.

The book was not in the library. They were sure of that after they'd looked along every shelf, turned round each of the books that was back to front, and removed them all to see if anything had got stuck behind. They did the same thing over again in Squire Thumping-Jolly's study. Drina longed to stop and read. *Stories of Lullwater Valley*, *Mysteries of Lullwater*, and *Tales of Carillon Castle* looked too fascinating to ignore, and she put them back with regret.

"Never mind," said Daffodil cheerfully. "There are more books all over the place."

"*More* books?" said Drina.

Billy rolled his eyes and Drina knew he'd rather be fishing.

Next they hunted through the Great Hall, the dining room and the kitchen, where the cat saw Jampot and leapt to the top of the dresser. Poodle knocked the bin

over and ate everything that fell out.

"Maybe it isn't here any longer," said Taffeta. She was gazing anxiously up at the cat, which had found a string of onions hanging from the ceiling and was clinging to it with all four paws. "Maybe it got thrown out."

"No," said Daffodil firmly. "They never throw anything out. I mean, except newspapers and used matches and bits of old candles and the paper that the fish comes wrapped in and empty flour bags and stuff that's really, really broken. And socks when Poodle's had them. They keep everything. Except..."

"Keep looking," said Billy.

Drina hunted through box after box of books, most of which were ancient recipes stained with butter and splashes of gravy. When they had finished in the kitchen and Taffeta had rescued the cat – and been scratched – they searched the bedrooms and landings. They even checked the pile of slightly damp books that Squire Thumping-Jolly liked to read in the bath.

It was no use, so they moved on to the attic where old furniture was stored. Dust blew up in grey clouds whenever they moved anything. Poodle stood at the door, sneezed, frightened himself and ran away, but Jampot stayed with them. Drina wished he hadn't because his fur was soon grey with dust.

"Is it me," said Drina, "or is everything in here a bit lopsided?"

"It's not you," said Daffodil. "Nothing in this house is absolutely straight. I mean, the furniture and things

43

are, but the walls aren't. It's because it's so old. It gets lopsided-er as you go up. There are sloping floors and the windows don't all shut properly so we have to stuff them with bits of cloth and twide and put things under the tables and the beds so that all the legs touch the floor, and when—"

There was a sudden shriek from Taffeta, then a giggle.

"I thought I saw a ghost," she said.

"Where?" demanded Drina, looking round.

"You," said Taffeta. "You're all grey and covered in dust and you looked just like a spookie. And Jampot looks like a ghost lion."

"They call them 'ooties' in Trabbershire," said Drina. "They take their ooties very seriously."

"Well, you look like an ootie then," said Taffeta.

"We all look like ooties," said Billy.

Taffeta gave a little bounce. "Ogging great ooties!" she said, and bent to look under the bed. "There's a book holding up a leg of this bed. Billy, can you lift the leg while I get it out?"

The book turned out to be *Diseases of Chickens – Volume Three*, which was disappointing. They pushed it back under the bed.

"But you might be on to something," said Drina. "Daffodil says they use things to prop up the legs of the furniture, so maybe that's where we should look."

They worked their way through the house once more. Most of the furniture was old, big and heavy, so it was a case of Drina, Daffodil and Billy heaving up

a corner of a wardrobe while Taffeta whipped out the book, reading the title aloud and pushing it back again. They found *Talking to Sheep* and *Diseases of Chickens – Volume Two,* but nothing to do with the Laws. Hot, grubby and tired, they sat down on the dining-room floor and Taffeta opened a window.

Something fell out.

"What was that?" asked Drina.

"Whatever was holding the window in place," said Daffodil. "I told you, the windows are wonky, so. . ."

"I mean, is it a book, and if it is, which one?" asked Drina.

"Volume One of *Diseases of–*" began Billy, but Drina had pounced on the book.

"This is it!" she cried.

The pages of *The Lullwater Laws* were old and fragile, and she handled them delicately. The book had become wet, so the print was blurred in places and the spine had almost rotted through, but when Drina set it gently on the table, they could still read it.

"Here's the bit about getting married!" said Drina. "And look at this bit" – she read aloud – *"The Lord of Lullwater shall own the land as described, but not the church, nor the dwellings."*

"Dwellings means houses, Taff," said Billy.

"I knew that," said Taffeta.

"And it says here," went on Drina, *"The Lord of Lullwater shall be an honest person and good to his people."*

"Some hope," said Billy.

Drina read on. *"The Lord shall own the Lullwater*

*Lake and all its pur . . . purtenances."*

"What's a purtenance?" asked Taffeta.

Daffodil, Drina and Billy looked at each other.

"Haven't a clue," said Billy.

"It sounds like a petticoat," said Taffeta.

"I don't think it can be," said Drina. *"The lake and all its petticoats* wouldn't make sense. Maybe it's the fish."

Jampot looked up.

"There's no such fish as a purtenance," said Daffodil. "Let's have a look, Drina."

"Oh, listen to this!" said Drina. *"If the people of Twidings claim that the Lord of Lullwater is not an honest man and is not keeping these Laws, they are to complain to the Quarter Court.* That means that if he does anything we don't like we just have to hold out until the next Quarter Court and complain. How much damage can he do in that time?"

"A lot, I should think," said Billy grimly. "Look at all those workmen he's got."

"And we still don't know what a purtenance is," said Taffeta.

"Granny would know," said Drina.

At the mention of Granny they all realized how tired, hot and dirty they were, so with the Squire's permission they took the book of *The Lullwater Laws* to show her.

On the way, they swam themselves clean in the lake (including Jampot, but not Poodle, who found a puddle to roll in so he could be dirty and wet at the same time). Jampot caught himself a fish and munched it contentedly as they dried off in the sun.

Drina lay with her head on Jampot's flank. There was nothing like a calm lion to help her think, and since coming to Twidings, Jampot seemed to be a very happy lion too. That had been a long swim, and she was sure his eyes were brighter than before.

"He loves it here," said Taffeta. "I wish you could both stay for ever." She covered her ears to shut out the noise of hammering from the castle. "Drina, where are you going?"

"To talk to your brothers," said Drina, and held out a hand to pull Taffeta to her feet. "Want to come?"

# Chapter Five

Billy and Taffeta's oldest brothers were Tweed and
Fustian. Drina explained her idea to them, then
together they went back to Granny's cottage to show
her the book.

"Purtenances sounds frilly," said Taffeta.

"Purtenances," said Granny, "are the things that
belong to something, or go with something."

"So the purtenances of the lake includes the reeds,
doesn't it?" said Drina.

"And the fish too," said Granny. "I'm afraid he owns
it all now."

"We should go reeding this afternoon then," said
Drina. "And fishing, before he can stop us. If we get
the reeds into the mecessaries and the fish into the
smokehouse, they'll keep."

"Granny," asked Taffeta, "do we really have to call him 'My Lord'?"

Granny did her sucking-a-lemon face again, but not for long. "Perhaps you do," she said. "But it depends on exactly what you mean by 'My Lord' when you say it. It could mean whatever you want it to mean. Now, off you go and do your reeding. Let me know how the work at the castle is going on."

"We will," said Taffeta innocently.

They walked to the shore, taking the long way round to see what was happening at the castle. It was surprising how many of the local men were helping with the rebuilding. Tweed and Fustian Fiddlestep were fitting a high window into place but it looked back to front so that it would only open from the outside. Bricks were sticking out at strange angles. Danny Goodenough, the vicar's son, was wheeling a barrow full of sand. He seemed to be holding firmly to the handles and looking where he was going, so how did he lose hold of it? Quite suddenly he'd dropped it, and the barrow somersaulted down the hill, sending a river of sand across the road.

"Oops," he said. "That'll take a while to sweep up. What a shame."

Drina smiled to herself.

All afternoon the children trailed along the shore carrying baskets of fish to the smokehouses and bundles of reeds to the mecessaries. Drina couldn't possibly carry all that fish about without giving some to Jampot, who was following her everywhere. Luckily

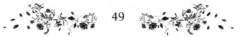

a few plump trout lasted him for a long time. At last, Billy shaded his eyes against the sun and squinted up at the church clock.

"It's after six," he said. "The men working on the castle will have gone home."

"I don't think so," said Drina. "They seemed very keen. Shall we go and see?"

They'd hardly started climbing the hill when they heard Gerbil shouting. Jampot placed himself in front of Drina. Approaching the castle, they saw that nobody was working any longer. It looked even more tumbledown than before. A whole row of stones had been put in sideways and stuck out over the walls. Through a window that didn't quite fit, Drina glimpsed a wooden floor so uneven that it made her seasick. The castle door was still leaning upside down against a wall, and even upside down it looked too small.

It was here that the workmen had gathered and Gerbil was shouting at everyone – but especially at the Fiddlestep boys.

"Idiots, fools!" he yelled. "You miserable creatures, you slime from the bottom of a drain, you repulsive pieces of vermin! Can't you even make a door that fits? What are you going to do next? Put the roof on upside down?"

"If you like, Mr Cravat," offered Fustian Fiddlestep.

"If you like, MY LORD!" stormed Gerbil. "And, no, My Lord does not like! My Lord wants workmen who know what they are doing! I never want to see you near my castle again!"

He flung out an arm to one side and Drina was afraid that he might hit someone, but he was only pointing away from the castle, to tell them to go. Everyone stepped back except Tweed Fiddlestep.

"Excuse me, *My Lord*," he said, "but who's going to build your castle when we're not here?"

Taffeta began to giggle and Drina nudged her.

"The men from Trabbershire can build it!" shrieked Gerbil. "I don't want to see you locals again! There are plenty of workers I can get in, men who really *want* to build my castle. You haven't seen what I can do! You haven't begun to see what I can do!"

Taffeta was laughing too much to stand. She had curled up on the ground, where spluttery noises escaped her. People were beginning to stare.

"Have you finished talking to us, My Lord?" asked Fustian pleasantly. "Shall we go away now?"

"OUT!!" screamed Gerbil.

The Fiddlestep boys and Danny Goodenough ran away laughing. Drina was sitting on the ground hugging Jampot and watching Taffeta rolling from side to side and turning purple when the sky darkened as if something had come in the way of the sun.

She looked up.

Gerbil was standing over them. For the first time, she noticed that one of his ears was flat against his head and the other stuck out.

"Good afternoon, My Lord," she said. A long squeal escaped from Taffeta.

"Why is that child laughing?" he demanded.

"She's not," said Drina quickly. "She's crying."

"Yes, she's crying," said Billy. He heaved Taffeta into his arms and held her against his shoulder where she shook in spasms. "You were shouting and it frightened her. There, there, little Taffy."

Gerbil looked as if he wasn't sure whether to believe them or not. "This village needs to look out," he said. "If you don't all start doing as you're told, you'll have something proper to cry about." And he strode away.

Taffeta sat up. She really was crying. She gulped and dried her tears on the back of her hands, laughed a bit more, then said, "I hurt."

"I'm not surprised," said Billy. "You nearly injured yourself."

"It's Granny's fault," she said, and hiccuped. "She said that 'My Lord' could mean whatever we want it to mean. So I decided it means 'you sweet little pumpkin'. It worked, didn't it, getting them to mess up the castle!"

"They've done it too well though," said Billy. "Now they've all been sacked and he's got new people coming in."

"We'll think of something," said Drina. She looked down at Jampot. He was gazing up at her. If you were a dog, she thought, you'd be wagging your tail.

More wagons arrived the next morning. This time they brought slates for the roof and wooden crates.

"There must be hundreds of them," said Drina.

"Thousands," said Taffeta.

"A sight too many," said Billy, as they watched from the treehouse. The men also unloaded a flagpole, but no flag. "It'll have a gerbil on it," said Billy.

"Mum asked if we'd take his new clothes up to him," said Taffeta. "They should be all parcelled up in an hour or two."

The parcels of clothes, wrapped up in brown paper, were heavy. They loaded them into Granny's wheelbarrow and trundled them up to the castle to find that it had a door now, a proper one that fitted. As well as the Trabbershire men there were more new workers, all wearing green shirts. The green-shirt people seemed to be in charge. One was guarding the door.

"Parcels for Mr Cravat," said Billy.

"To be delivered in person," said Drina. "We have to give them to Mr Cravat."

"I'll take them," said a woman in a green shirt. Jampot growled, and the Green-Shirt Woman looked as if she might growl back. "Lose yourselves," she said.

Billy shrugged. "We may as well go to the mecessaries," he said. "There are all those reeds we took yesterday, they need preparing. Dad says there's been a big order for squashed up twide to make paper."

Mecessary Number Three was a shed on the lake shore. It was painted red, with double doors at each end, and inside lay heaps of fresh damp reeds. Billy and Drina spread them out and Jampot sat down to watch.

Drina and Taffeta walked barefoot over the bumpy stems, which were pleasantly smooth and dangerously slippery.

"Don't worry," said Billy. "The doors at the lake end are open. If you slipped you'd just slide straight out of the mecessary, like sledging. You might stop before you reached the water – or you might not."

"I like to flop on them," said Taffeta. She flung herself face down on the reeds and rolled in them. "It doesn't matter what you do so long as they get squished, but you have to soften them without breaking them up."

"Drina's been in mecessaries before," said Billy. "She knows what to do."

"But it's been a long time," said Drina. She copied Taffeta and rolled over in the cool damp reeds.

"That's lovely!" she said. "Like a cool swim! I'm surprised Mr Day hasn't invented something to do this. But I'm glad he didn't."

"He did," said Billy, stamping. "But nobody used it because it's more fun this way. Drina, what's Jampot doing?"

They sat up, wet and reedy, to watch him. Jampot was walking steadily across the reeds towards Drina.

"Get him out," said Billy sharply. "He'll break them."

"No, he won't," said Drina, watching. "He has velvety paws. He's a cat, and cats walk gently."

Taffeta sat up. "She's right," she said. "He hasn't broken any. They're just nicely flattened."

Jampot lay down among the reeds and wondered

where this wonderful stuff had been all his life. He closed his eyes blissfully, and rolled.

Billy sighed loudly.

"It's all right," said Drina softly. "He's not damaging them. They're perfectly squished."

"He can squish more reeds than Drina and I can, in no time," added Taffeta. "And he's enjoying it so much!"

The mecessary doors crashed open.

Daffodil's voice thundered over them. "GUESS WHAT!" she bellowed.

"No!" yelled Billy, but it was too late. Poodle was bounding through the mecessary. For a terrible moment it looked as if all four legs would splay in different directions, but somehow they caught up with each other and he was sitting down by the time he slid out of the doors at the other end. Jampot sat up in surprise.

"Daffodil," said Billy wearily, "did you have to bring him in here?"

"It's not my fault," she said. "You should have shut the door."

Far away there was a splash and a wet bark. "It could have been anyone who sailed through there; me or your granny or, or, or . . . anyone. Anyway, Jampot's in here."

"Jampot's not an idiot," said Billy.

"If you're going to be like that, I won't tell you," said Daffodil crossly.

Drina picked herself up and carefully removed the bits of reed from Taffeta's hair. "Billy didn't mean to be cross," she said gently. "He just didn't want Poodle to get hurt." *He didn't want a mecessary full of broken reeds*

*and dog hairs either*, she thought, but she wasn't going to mention that.

"Gerbil's put his flag up!" said Daffodil. "And it's . . . it's like . . . it's. . ."

"Has it got a gerbil on it?" asked Taffeta hopefully.

"A coat of arms?" asked Drina.

"Oh, a moustache?" said Taffeta.

"No, it's—"

"NO!" shouted Billy for the second time that day, and ran over the reeds to shut the lake-end doors. Drina was just in time to see Poodle, who had swum ashore, galloping towards them, streaming with waterweed. Billy got there first and slammed the doors shut, and there was a thud of something wet, fast and very big hitting them from outside.

"It won't hurt him," said Billy. "Now, tell us about this banner."

"It's blue on a white background," began Daffodil, "and it's got his initials in the middle. But you should see what he's got over that! It's a giganormous crown, with, you know, a sort of rounded top and everything, just like a real one!"

"So he thinks he's king over us all," said Billy. "We already knew that."

"And there's something else underneath," she went on.

"Yes?" said Drina.

"And it's – well, I don't really know what it is."

Taffeta flopped back into the reeds again.

"Nobody can tell," said Daffodil. "It looks a bit like a

letter *T*. A capital letter *T*. Except one end looks bent. Do you think it means Gerbil the Terrible? Or Gerbil the Tempestuous?"

"The Tyrant," said Drina, hugging Jampot.

"What's a . . . what you said?" asked Taffeta.

"A tyrant is somebody who makes harsh laws and forces people to obey them," said Drina. "It means nobody has any freedom..." Suddenly she had to hide her face in Jampot's mane until she knew that she wouldn't cry. Twidings-on-Lullwater had been the loveliest place she knew, full of uncomplicated people who went about their business and helped each other. Gerbil was destroying it. Jampot licked her arm to comfort her.

"It'll be all right, Drina," said Billy. "We just have to wait until the next Quarter Court, then we can get him out."

"I don't think it'll be that simple," said Drina. "He has a book of *The Lullwater Laws*, he *knows* that he can be kicked out by the Quarter Court judge. I expect he's already thinking of ways round it."

Taffeta pulled herself up from the reeds. "Shall we go up to the castle and look at this flag?" she said.

Outside the mecessary, Poodle was waiting for Daffodil to come out so that he could put his paws on her shoulders. He was still dripping wet and covered in waterweed.

"That dog," sighed Billy. "It hasn't the sense to shake itself. Castle, then."

\*

At the castle they found quite a gathering of Twidings people, including Granny, shading their eyes to gaze up at the flag fluttering over the rebuilt battlements. It was white, with the imposing crown over Gerbil's initials.

"You see," said Daffodil. "A letter *T* for Gerbil the Terrible."

"It could be an umbrella," observed Taffeta, and tipped her head to one side thoughtfully. "Or a tree. With a flat top."

Drina stepped closer to Billy. "What do you think?" she asked quietly. "I mean, I know what I think, but I might be wrong."

"It's a hammer," he said.

"That's what I thought," said Drina. "Is that what he wants to be? The Hammer of Twidings? Beating us all down?"

Jampot put his paw on Drina's leg and growled. Gerbil was behind them, wearing the usual grey suit with a high-collared cloak of black velvet over it. His black boots reached above his knees and must have had soft soles for him to creep up on them so quietly. A gold lining gleamed from inside his cloak.

Taffeta's eyes sparkled with laughter.

"A hammer, indeed," said Gerbil, and with a flourish he raised his hand. He was holding a hammer that looked very new and a bit dangerous.

"And what do we use hammers for, Miss Snapdragon?" he asked.

"For putting nails in," said Drina, and added, "My – er – Lord." She didn't dare look at Taffeta.

Gerbil frowned and his moustache stuck out.

"For building, child," he said. "It is a sign of building, and I intend to have a lot of building done in this village. There will be changes here. You won't recognize the place."

"But we love it the way it is," said Daffodil.

He smiled unpleasantly down at her. "But it isn't up to you, is it, Daffodil? It's up to me. All that happens here will be up to me. I do hope we can all work happily together."

Unfortunately, at that moment, Poodle remembered something. He remembered to shake himself.

As Drina said afterwards, the spray of grey hair, mud, sand grit, reedy bits, twigs and small dead fish didn't only fall on Gerbil. Everybody got some. But while most people went away and washed it off in the lake, Gerbil threw back his long black cloak with a flash of golden lining, raising the hammer high in the air.

"From now on," he screamed, "all dogs must be kept on leads at all times! *Short* leads! And the same applies to lions! I make the laws in this village, so make sure you obey me! Obey me, you minions and underlings!"

Granny tossed her head so that the blue butterflies in her hair shone in the sunlight, turned her back on Gerbil and walked briskly back to her cottage. The children followed her, and Drina spent the evening making a beautiful lead for Jampot out of plaited twide, as well as finishing off Granny's sewing projects and picking up hairpins.

Gerbil marched to the castle, shedding damp dog

hair and green bits. Muttering bitterly to himself, he made a vow. He would not stop until he had made these people so terrified that they would obey him in every single little thing. Being the Lord of Lullwater was not enough. He would be the Hammer of Lullwater.

# Chapter Six

The sound of hammering woke Drina the next morning. She hid her head under the covers, tried to go back to sleep, and nearly managed it, but just when the hammers had stopped for a minute or two they began again.

She sat up. "Jampot?" she said.

He was at the window with both front paws on the sill. She knelt beside him. Everywhere, wagons were being unloaded. Along the lake shore, men in vests and shorts were hammering posts into the ground with the ones in green shirts giving orders.

Granny appeared on the landing in her dressing gown. "What's happening?" she called. "Drina, my dear, what do those men think they're doing? Are they building a fence?"

"I'll find out," said Drina, and pulled her clothes on. "Jampot, stay. Guard Granny. Good lion." If the workmen saw a lion they'd probably want to run away and climb up a tree, which would be silly because lions can climb trees too.

She ran to the shore, watched for a minute or two, then asked, "What are you making?"

"Nothing to do with little girls," said a Green-Shirt Man.

Drina didn't mind being called "ginger" or "young Snapdragon", but "little girl" offended her very much. Perhaps she should have brought Jampot after all. She was about to say that she couldn't see any little girls when Taffeta came running to meet her, her hair messy and flying around her face.

"We were looking out from the treehouse," she said, a bit out of breath from running. "Billy thinks they're going to build a fence round the lake."

"Well, that's ogging clever of him, because that's exactly what we're doing," said one of the Trabbershire men.

The man in the green shirt glared at him. "You've been told before, you're not paid to chat to the local kids," he said. "Lord Cravat gave orders about that."

"But he can't!" said Taffeta. "The lake is everybody's!"

"It's Gerbil's now," said Drina, but she wished Jampot was there to lean against her leg and reassure her. Not having the lake would be like not having a heart. "And what's going on round the castle?"

Lengths of pale-green canvas were spread on the grass. People were fitting poles together.

"They're pitching tents!" she exclaimed, then added, "Of course!"

More workmen were arriving all the time, and a lot of them were from Trabbershire. They couldn't go home every night, and there wouldn't be enough room for them to stay in the village or even sleep in the wagons. There would have to be a camp.

She stepped to one side to let a horse-drawn wagon through. It was loaded with fence posts longer than the wagon itself.

"Them's the ogging great posts you wanted, sir," said the Trabbershire man, and climbed on a chair. "You kids, will you hold this while I hammer it in?"

Drina and Taffeta quickly turned and walked away.

They were making breakfast when Daffodil arrived with Poodle, who was on a lead and trying to eat it. A fresh warm smell of bread came from the covered basket on her arm.

"Mummy said to bring you some loaves," she said. "I told her I was coming to see you this morning and she asked me to take some bread because the village is so full of people doing building and they'd buy all the bread in the bakery and there wouldn't be any left for the people who live here."

"I never thought of that," said Drina.

"Gerbil must provide their food, surely?" observed Granny Annie. "We're a generous village, but there isn't enough food in Twidings for such a horde."

They were all silent for a while, looking down at the

 63

warm bread and butter. It hadn't occurred to any of them that with Gerbil and his workforce around, there might not be enough to eat.

"Would Gerbil make the local people go hungry?" asked Drina.

"He doesn't like the local people," said Taffeta with a pout. "He called us onions and underpants."

"I'm sure he didn't," said Daffodil. "He called us lots of things, but he didn't called us onions. Anyway, we're not onions; we're not round and we don't smell like soup and make people cry. . ."

They buttered their rolls while Taffeta argued that Mr Pongo the gravedigger was round and smelt of soup and he made Linen cry once when he stepped on her foot, and finally Drina remembered that, the day before, Gerbil had called them "minions and underlings", and while they were explaining to Taffeta that minions and underlings was not a nice thing to call people but it wasn't the same as onions and underpants, Billy arrived, so the whole conversation had to be repeated.

"*Nobody* shall go hungry," said Granny. "Whoever they are. I'm sure we can think of something."

As she wasn't doing her sucking-a-lemon face, she clearly wasn't going to do the thinking herself. She was looking at Drina.

"We will," said Drina.

"And before we do another thing," went on Granny, "let's look at *The Lullwater Laws*. I think it's on page five. Read it out for me, Drina, I don't know what I've done with my glasses."

Drina wiped the butter from her fingers and read from page five: *"All villagers of Twidings-on-Lullwater shall have access to the lake and its shore at all times. All villagers must be free to take fish, rushes, reeds, weeds and watercress from Lullwater Lake."*

"We can't do that with a fence in the way," said Drina. "Does that mean he has to stop building?"

"We'll have to challenge him about it," said Granny.

"At least nobody will marry him," Taffeta pointed out. "He even proposed to Widow Grind-Spirtle and she banged the door in his face, so he went next door and proposed to her mum."

"Did she shut the door in his face too?" asked Granny.

"No, she's deaf, so she didn't know what he was talking about. She thought he was the undertaker coming to see if she was dead. She chased him down the path with a broom. Nobody will have him."

They were interrupted by the clanging of a bell so loud and so flat that everybody winced and covered their ears. Jampot put his paws on the windowsill and growled, and Poodle hid under the table. Daffodil held her hands over his ears.

"Is something on fire?" asked Granny.

Billy looked outside. "Everyone's running to the Village Green," he said. "We'd better go and see what's happening."

The Village Green was crowded when they got there. A platform had been built so that everyone could see Gerbil, who was sitting at a table with the velvet cloak over his suit.

65

"It's such a sunny day!" whispered Taffeta. "He must be boiling!"

"He looks ridiculous," Granny whispered back.

Drina wasn't sure. He did look ridiculous but he looked dangerous too. Two men in dark-green shirts, black trousers and shiny boots were striding about. One had the bell in his hand and both of them were shouting.

"Village Green!" they bellowed. "Everybody to the Village Green!"

"There's another Green-Shirt Man behind Gerbil," said Daffodil.

"And another one bringing everyone from the shore, but she's a woman," said Taffeta.

The four people in dark-green shirts herded everyone to the Village Green, which wasn't difficult because they all wanted to know what was going on. Men, women and children streamed in from the mecessaries, the houses and the shops. Squire Thumping-Jolly and the Honourable Veronica were on their way down from Thumping Old Hall. The vicar, the Reverend Benedict Goodenough, and his family came from the vicarage. Little Mrs Baggotty and her enormous sons turned up, and all the Fiddlesteps arrived with their sewing in their hands. Widow Grind-Spirtle brought a poker in case Gerbil tried to marry her and her mother brought the broom in case he tried to bury her. The young women stayed as far back as possible.

Gerbil smiled, which was frightening. The people in

the dark-green shirts lined up behind him. They were all tall and broad-shouldered with very short hair.

"Good morning, my people," said Gerbil, beaming round at them all. "I have called you here today to tell you how we will work together to make this village the most remarkable place in the country."

"It already is," said Drina. She hadn't meant to say it aloud, it just came out.

"Be quiet, Andrina Snapdragon," ordered Gerbil.

"I didn't say a word!" said Granny Annie.

"*And* you, Andrina Snapdragon!" said Gerbil, and continued, "We will be quite wonderfully famous. Everybody will know about us."

"We don't want to be famous!" said somebody in the crowd.

"You weren't asked," said Gerbil. "But I'm sure you'll all come to see things my way. My plan is to make Twidings an exciting lakeside holiday resort. There will be two hotels beside the lake and holiday homes on the hillside. Another hotel will be built when we've cut down all those trees in the wood."

"Billy's house!" gasped Taffeta, and reached for his hand.

"We will have swimming pools..."

"We've got a lake," muttered Billy.

"...and pleasure boats, cafés and hairdressers. This is great news for you all! Our visitors will need to have their rooms cleaned. They will need to eat. You can all be cooks, waiters and cleaners. You can take our tourists for trips round the lake. You can do their

washing. I will open shops where they can spend their money. There will be plenty of work for us all."

Granny raised her good hand. "Excuse me, Mr Cravat," she said, "but we already have plenty of work. If we're working in your hotels we won't have time to fish, or harvest reeds and make things out of them, as we've always done."

Gerbil made a thin little noise. It sounded like a door creaking. Taffeta looked nervously up at Drina. "Was that laughing?" she asked.

"Yes, I think so," answered Drina.

"You don't need all that old stuff!" creaked Gerbil. "All that messing about with water and reeds. I will give you proper work! I have brought the future to Twidings-on-Lullwater!"

"We don't want it!" shouted Veronica Thumping-Jolly.

"We have workmen from Trabbershire to do the building," said Gerbil, "And to help me to keep everything running smoothly, I have brought in my very special team. You will recognize them by their green shirts. Behind me, in the dark-green shirts, are my special assistants, Harry, Gary, Barry and Wendy-Jane. They are here to help you."

The Dark-Green-Shirt people all nodded without smiling.

"Believe me," said Gerbil, "I care passionately about this village! I care so much that I want nothing but the best for Twidings. And I know what the best is. WHAT?"

The "WHAT" was because Granny had raised her hand again.

"Mr Cravat," she said, "pardon me, but it is in *The Lullwater Laws* that everyone in the village must have access to the shore and the lake. You appear to be building a very tall fence. We can't get down to the shore with that in the way."

"Then I must remind you of another law," he said firmly. "The Lord of Lullwater owns all purtenances of the lake. The fish are mine. So are the reeds."

"And yet the law also gives us the right to take them," Granny pointed out.

Daffodil raised her hand too. "And all the other things that you find by the lake," she said. "You get pebbles and shells there, and driftwood washed up and you can make things out of that, and once I found a bottle with a message in it and the message was all wet and my brother Tarquin said..."

Gerbil raised both his hands. "My dear girl!" he exclaimed. "Do you think I'm an unreasonable man? I am making arrangements to protect your rights. I will permit all of you to take fish and reeds from the lake!"

"I should think so!" said Granny.

"Permits will be on sale as soon as the fence is finished," he said. "A fishing permit will cost only four guineas, and that will last for a whole six months. Three guineas for a reeding permit, and you kiddies can have one for half price! Little Miss Thumping-Jolly, I had not thought about permits for picking up shells and

driftwood, but I suppose two guineas for adults and one for children should be fair."

The crowd were muttering. Harry and Barry left Gerbil's platform and walked slowly towards the villagers. Jampot pressed so close to Drina that he nearly pushed her over, and she kept a hand on his mane. The crowd grumbled. Then Benedict Goodenough, who was thin and a bit scruffy with straggly hair, stepped forward and turned to face them.

"Twiders!" he called. "I know what you are thinking. You are thinking that Mr Cravat is behaving like a tyrant. You are right. Perhaps some of you are also thinking of picking him up and throwing him in the lake, and his hideous new fence after him. But it would only make things worse. We don't want the Lord of Lullwater to charge us with assault and vandalism, do we? Let's wait for the Quarter Court, and we can charge him with being the worst Lord of Lullwater anybody could imagine." He turned and looked Gerbil in the eyes. "And as for you, I don't know how you can sleep at night!"

Gerbil smiled again. "One more word out of you, vicar," he said, "and I will build you your very own prison cell in the castle, where *you* won't sleep at all." He stood up. "I have to leave the village for a while."

There was a gasp, then silence. It sounded as if everyone had been about to cheer, then decided it would be better not to.

"In the meantime, work will go on," he said. "If you

have any questions, Harry, Barry, Gary and Wendy-Jane will be delighted to help you. Absolutely delighted."

People began to drift away, glancing over their shoulders at Gerbil and his Green Shirts. Daffodil went home with her parents, who were talking about making soup and scones for everyone because there was still food at the Hall and the shops were empty. Taffeta offered to help. And Drina had an idea.

# Chapter Seven

On warm summer evenings in Twidings-on-Lullwater villagers liked to gather on the shore or the Village Green. Mostly they would take "something to be going on with", which meant a bit of knitting or sewing or a piece of driftwood to carve. If any musicians were around, or somebody with a good voice like Benedict Goodenough, there'd be singing and dancing. Children played games. There was a patch of bare ground in the middle of the green where the maypole went up for May Day, and at other times it was a good place for a cooking fire.

This evening nobody felt much like singing, dancing or playing. No one could get near the lake, and wherever you looked there was somebody in a green shirt, watching. Only the workmen had gathered on the

Village Green when Drina, Billy and Granny arrived. They carried armfuls of dried reeds and a metal bucket half full of water. Jampot trotted beside them.

"He looks younger all of a sudden," observed Granny.

"He sort of is," said Drina, who had noticed the same thing. "He trots instead of plodding. The air and the water here are so good for him."

As well as reeds they had brought a few other useful things – pebbles and shells from Granny's garden, a few dead flowers, sand, fish bones, a pair of worn-out old leather boots that had belonged to all the Fiddlestep girls in turn and were now too small even for Taffeta, feathers, clippings from Jampot's mane, orange peel and a dead beetle. Drina and Billy had argued because Billy thought they should take worms and sheep droppings too, and Drina had refused. She'd only just agreed to the fish bones and the beetle.

On the scorched, ashy square in the middle of the Green, they kindled a fire with sticks they'd picked in the wood and set the bucket over it. Jampot lay in the warmth to watch the fire and Billy sat beside him, shredding reeds with his penknife and dropping them into the bucket. Drina stirred in some sand, then crushed the fish bones with pebbles and threw those in too.

"You'll have to cut them thinner than that, Billy," she said, just loudly enough for anyone around to hear. "They're tough; they'll never soften if you put them in too big." She took one of the boots and banged it with a stone, and Taffeta got to work with the other one.

"Excuse me," said one of the workmen, "what are you doing?"

Drina pushed the hair back from her face. "Softening the leather," she said. "Billy, can I borrow your knife?"

Billy wiped the knife on the grass and passed it to her. She cut a thin slice of leather from the rotting old boot and pounded it even harder. Taffeta sprinkled sand into the bucket.

The workmen were all watching now. So were the Green Shirts. Finally, a Trabbershire man asked, "What are you making?"

"Tough Stew," said Billy promptly.

"But it's not. . ." began one of the men – he had very short hair and an earring – ". . .not the sort of stew that you eat, is it?"

"Course you eat it, that's why it's called stew," said Billy. "What else would you do with it? I mean, apart from fertiliser. You can use it for that if you strain the stones out first."

Drina threw in some flower heads and prodded them down with a stick. It was bubbling now, and green froth was forming on the top.

"So they taste all right, do they, those reeds?" asked the man.

"They taste terrible," said Billy. "Want to try one?"

"No, thanks," said the man, but one of his friends took one and bit into it. He pulled a face like a baby about to scream, and wiped his mouth on the back of his hand.

"They're not so bad when they've simmered for a few

days," said Billy sympathetically. "And when you've put in plenty of other stuff to disguise the taste."

Drina added a handful of orange peel. "It still needs more reeds," she said. "And a lot more leather."

"And some shee—" began Billy.

"No, it doesn't," said Drina quickly.

"Leather?" asked somebody.

"For protein," explained Drina, stirring the stew.

"No wonder you call it Tough Stew," said the man with the earring.

"Oh, that doesn't mean it's tough to eat," said Drina. "Well, apart from the leather. It's what we eat when times are tough and there isn't enough food to go round."

Billy added the beetle. "There's only one beetle, I'm afraid," he said. "The sparrow got the rest. Any more fish bones, Taffy?"

"But times aren't hard, are they?" asked the earring man. "Isn't there enough food in this place?"

"Course there isn't!" said Billy. "Not with all these extra people! I mean, nothing against you, but with all of you builders and carpenters and all that, we'll soon run out. If we put the stew on now and leave it to simmer overnight. . ."

". . .and the next day," said Taffeta.

". . .and the day after that, and with more leather it'll be – well, at least it won't taste of reeds."

"It'll taste of Taffy's old boot more than anything," said Drina. She nestled against Jampot and watched the steam rising from the pot. "Orangey old boot. It doesn't sound very nice, but by the time we get to eating Tough Stew we're glad to eat anything."

The greenish foam on the top was turning grey and scummy. Several of the men were backing away.

"I think we should speak to Harry about this," said the earring man to the people who were nearest. "Or Gary, or Barry, or Wendy-Jane. One of the people in charge. We need to make sure we get all our food brought in, and plenty of it."

"Oh, you're most welcome to share the Tough Stew!" said Drina. "If we run out of fresh reeds we can always use dried ones. There are plenty of those because we use them to make carpets."

"And I can find more beetles," said Billy. "Big, shiny, crunchy ones."

Earring had turned the same colour as the scum on the top of the bucket. He put his hand over his mouth.

"Well, this has been delightful," said Granny, "cooking out of doors is such a pleasant thing to do, but the fire is dying down now and it's getting dark. Let's go home and put the stew on the stove. I still have a little firewood left."

"Yes, Granny," said Drina obediently.

Taffeta gathered up the remaining bits of reed, pebbles, and anything that hadn't ended up in the stew and Drina and Billy carried the bucket home between them. Glancing back over her shoulder, Drina saw the man with the earring and several of his friends talking urgently to Harry and Barry.

"Good," she said. "They won't want to eat village food now. Granny, what shall we do with this?"

"Let it cool down and pour it on the roses," advised Granny. "Well done, everyone! That was very successful."

"It would have worked even better with shee—" began Billy.

"No, it wouldn't," said Drina, "and we mustn't be too pleased with ourselves. We won this time, but we don't know what will happen next. I wonder why Gerbil went away?" She looked out of the window. "There's nobody there at the fence just now. I'll see if I can slip down there with Jampot." If Gerbil was going to stop them getting to the lake, Jampot must enjoy it while he could.

Drina sat on a rock splashing her feet in the water and watched Jampot swim. It was as if Lullwater Lake was washing years away from Jampot, and not just any years – it was washing away the years when he had been hungry and neglected, and badly used. He became stronger, healthier and happier with every day, and the thought of losing all this was unbearable. She didn't like thinking about going home to the circus either.

A few mornings later Drina stood with Granny outside the cottage, staring in disbelief at the fence. It was now twice the height of a tall man and reinforced with corrugated iron, and reached as far as they could see in either direction. Worse, building had started on the hotel and the air was filled with dust.

They did what they knew everyone else would be doing – walked to the Village Green to get a better view and talk about how terrible it all was.

Most of the Twidings people had assembled. Billy and Taffeta were there with all their brothers and sisters and their parents, who were Drina's Aunt Jemima and Uncle Tam. Aunt Jemima was little and delicate-looking, like Granny Annie, with the same red hair as Drina and mischievous eyes like Taffeta's. Uncle Tam was a wiry man with curly hair that was growing grey and a look about him that was sharp as scissors and as piercing as a needle. Aunt Jemima, Uncle Tam and the older Fiddlesteps had tape measures round their necks and pincushions on their sleeves. Aunt Jemima was crocheting lace as she looked up at the fence. Velvet Fiddlestep was pinning ribbon to a bonnet.

Jampot licked Drina and wished he could do more to help. And it had all being going so well, he thought sadly. He had felt younger and stronger since he came here.

"You can see that fence from my tree," said Billy. "It must go half a mile down either side of the lake at least."

"There must be a way through," said Drina. "He said we could get reeding permits."

"There," said Billy, pointing. "And there. We have doors."

Drina could hardly see the doors in the fence because the Green Shirts were standing in front of them. A large sign had been put up:

NO ACCESS TO THE LAKE WITHOUT A PERMIT. PERMITS FOR UP TO SIX MONTHS CAN BE BOUGHT AT THE CASTLE BETWEEN THE HOURS OF NINE AND FIVE, MONDAY TO FRIDAY, AT THE FOLLOWING PRICES:

| | |
|---|---|
| Fishing | four guineas for adults |
| Reeding | three guineas for adults<br>Half price for children<br>under fourteen |
| Beachcombing and<br>anything else | two guineas for adults<br>Half price for children |
| All other activities | see Fishing and Reeding |

FOR VISITORS TO GRAND CRAVAT LULLWATER LAKE HOLIDAY CENTRE, ENTRANCE IS FREE.

"He's really done it," said Billy, folding his arms. "He's come between us and the lake. We can't even see it."

"Isn't there a way round?" asked Drina.

"No," said Daffodil flatly. "I looked down from the Hall and it's even higher on that side, and they've got guards at each end of the fence so you can't get round and that's what I was going to do because Poodle likes to go for a swim and so do I, and I didn't see why we should miss our swim just because of Gerbil when

79

we've always lived here and he's only just come and it's not as if—"

"Thanks, Daffodil," said Billy.

"Only I thought you'd like to know," said Daffodil rather huffily. "Oh, what's *she* doing here?"

Wendy-Jane had arrived, elbowing her way past Uncle Tam and looking up at the fence with approval. The chatter of conversation stopped. Jampot growled.

"That looks solid," she said. "If you want permits, go to the castle for them."

Granny reached for her purse and Uncle Tam was opening his wallet. There was a bit of quiet conversation between them about who would pay for what, and money was slipped into Billy and Drina's hands.

"You'll need permits for yourselves, Taffeta and me," said Granny. "That man won't keep the Snapdragons from Lullwater Lake."

"What about lions?" asked Drina.

"And dogs?" said Daffodil.

"Did I hear 'lions and dogs'?" demanded Wendy-Jane in a voice that made everyone stop talking and pay attention. "What do you think this is, a circus?"

"Well, as you mention it—" began Daffodil, but Drina elbowed her and she stopped.

"Visitors to Lord Cravat's hotel don't want to find your mutt running about," said Wendy-Jane. "And as for lions, I wondered what that moth-eaten, smelly old thing was. Who wants to see that on the shore?"

She strode away. Drina folded her arms round

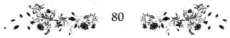

Jampot and buried her face in his mane. Jampot nuzzled her back. If he could have hugged her, he would.

Billy sat beside Drina and put a hand on her shoulder. When she looked up her eyes were pink, but Billy pretended not to notice.

"Don't listen to her," he said. "What does she know about lions?"

"He's not moth-eaten and he's not smelly," she said. "At least, only his breath is, and that isn't as bad as it used to be. He's better since he's been here. I thought he was just getting old and that was why he plodded round everywhere and looked dull. Then we came to Twidings and a few days of lake air, and swimming, and fish have made him younger. That's why I wanted to get him a permit, because the lake's so good for him."

"We'll find a way to get him some fish," said Billy. "We'd better go for our permits; there's already a queue. It's mostly children. Maybe the adults can't afford the grown-up permits."

The sun grew hot as they stood in the long queue, and sweat trickled down Drina's back. Jampot panted in the heat. When their turn came at last, the Green Shirt at the desk wrote out permits for the Fiddlesteps and Granny, then turned to Drina.

"Elizabeth Andrina Snapdragon," said Drina. "I live at Water's Edge Cottage."

The Green-Shirt Woman looked hard at Drina, then turned to say something quietly to the woman next to her. Presently one of the Dark Greens – Drina thought

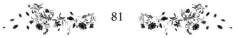

it was Gary, but it might have been Harry or Barry – appeared and spoke in whispers to the two Green-Shirt Women, glancing at Drina.

The Green-Shirt Woman sighed deeply, tore up the paper and started again.

"Elizabeth Andrina Snapdragon," she said sternly. "Your real address, please? Because you don't actually live at Water's Edge Cottage, do you?"

"I do when I'm here," said Drina. "And I'm here all summer."

"Exactly," said the woman. "*Home* address?"

It was a question Drina always dreaded. Fortunately she wasn't asked it very often.

"Snapdragon Family Circus," she said.

The woman smiled sweetly as if she were speaking to a very small child. "And can you tell me the address of Snapdragon Family Circus?"

Drina looked her in the eyes. "Wherever we happen to be," she said. "We're very popular. At this time of year the circus is usually not very far from Carillon."

"And that's not in Twidings," said the woman. "Next?"

"But my family—" began Drina.

The woman ignored her. She was looking past Drina at the child who came next in the queue.

"Name?" she asked.

Billy and Drina walked silently down to the Village Green. Granny was there, and the usual mix of Twidings people and workmen. They sat watching

the long queues of people, mostly children, lining up to show their permits to the stern-faced guards at the gates. The sight of Jampot's wise, gentle face looking hopefully up at her was more than Drina could bear, and she hid her face in his mane.

"I'm sorry, Jampot," she said. "I couldn't get you a permit, and you love the lake so much."

"Are you all right?" asked Billy.

She pulled up a few blades of grass and twisted them in her fingers.

"I've never been made to feel like an outsider in Twidings before," she said. "That's all." She folded her lips tightly and squeezed her eyes shut for a few seconds, and then she was able to go on. "All those people who come to his hotels, they'll be able to wander down to the lake whenever they feel like it, and we have to stay away."

"I should think so," said a voice behind them.

Drina looked round to see Godric Baggotty, a blond young man who repaired boats. "They'll pay that much for staying in those hotels, they'll want the lake to themselves. Still, as Lord Cravat said, there'll be plenty of work."

"There already is work," said Billy.

"Different work," said Godric. "We won't be stuck with making a living off the lake now. There's plenty of Twidings people went away to find work somewhere else. My sister, Twinkle, she went to sell clothes in one of those posh shops somewhere. Mind, she never liked it much in Twidings."

Drina thought about this. New people came to the village; others left to do something different. That was all right. Her father had left the village to join a circus and her Auntie Haf had moved to Africa because she wanted to look after elephants. Having a hotel in the village was all right too – but not like this, a monstrosity of a building designed to make money for a monstrosity of a Lord of Lullwater and steal the lake from the Twider people.

"It shouldn't be like this," she said.

"No it ogging well shouldn't," said someone else, and she turned to see one of the Trabbershire men standing behind her. "If Mr Cravat—"

"The Lord of Lullwater," put in somebody in a green shirt. They seemed to be everywhere now.

"If His Lordship wants a hotel, that's fair enough," said the Trabbershire man. "But if he wants it ready and open before the end of the summer, he's making a mistake. You can't build a hotel properly in that time. It'll be a botched-up, shoddy job if it's done too quickly."

"Have you told him that?" asked Billy.

"I told that Barry or Larry or Gary or whatever his name is," said the man. "I told him; I said it can't be done in that time, not properly, and you can't expect the lads to go on working halfway through the night when it's dark and all. And you know what he said? He said, 'You're a good worker, Mr Clark, and we'd be sorry to lose you.' In other words, I have to do as I'm told or I'll be sacked. And he's said the same to any number of the other lads too."

Drina was still cross about the permits. She wasn't in a mood to hear more. "Then you should all stand up to him," she said. "Why build it when you know it's rubbish?"

Granny had been sitting so quietly that Drina had thought she was asleep, but now, she said, "I'm very sorry to hear of your problems, Mr – Clark, is it?"

"Clarkie, madam, that's me," said the Trabbershire man.

Granny nodded and got to her feet. "Drina," she said firmly, "I should like to go home. Will you come with me, dear?"

They went home with Jampot running ahead. When the cottage door was shut behind them, Granny said, "You were quite snappy just now, Drina, with that Trabbershire man – Clarkie, I should say."

"Of course I was snappy!" said Drina. "They're doing whatever Gerbil wants and it's ruining our village! What with the Green Shirts listening to everything you say and the workmen putting up fences and scaffolding everywhere, there's nowhere safe where we can just – just go and be normal! They won't even let me go to the lake shore!"

"All the same," said Granny. "You can show them simple politeness."

"Certainly not," said Drina.

"Elizabeth Andrina," said Granny with a sigh, "would you like any of them to show a little sense or kindness? Would you like any of them to be helpful to you? Would you like to be allowed near the lake?"

"Of course I would," said Drina a bit crossly.

"Then don't make enemies," said Granny. "Those Green Shirt people are rather sinister, but the Trabbershire men are simply trying to earn all the money they can to take home to their families so that they can get through the winter. Mr Clarkie, for example. We should invite him and some friends to tea. It's no good being mean to somebody today when you might need their help tomorrow."

Later that afternoon Drina stood by the fence waiting for Billy and Taffeta to come back from the lake. Jampot pawed at the ground, then at the fence, then at Drina.

"I know," she said. "You want to go to the water and so do I, and you can't understand why not. Let's look for Taffeta, shall we? Is she coming?"

Children were leaving the shore, trailing through the narrow gates with meagre bags of reeds and not much fish. Each one looked hot, tired and dejected. Even Billy and Taffeta looked glum when they finally appeared, though Taffeta's face lit up when she saw Jampot. She flopped down beside him and took a fish from her basket.

"There's not much," she said. "But you need your fish, don't you, Jampot?"

"We had to go out a long way to get any," explained Billy as Jampot gobbled down the fish and licked Taffeta's hands. "There's hardly any near the shore, only a few titchy little ones. And some of them were already

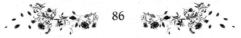

86

dead, so we weren't touching those. All this hammering is driving them away, and goodness knows what's going into our lake. Even further out, there weren't as many as there should be."

"There weren't many reeds at this end of the lake either," said Taffeta. "I mean, there were, but they were all covered in sawdust and brick dust and everything dust, and they'd gone all limp and useless. It's been a rubbish day. What have you been doing?"

"Not much," said Drina. "I had to invite one of the Trabbershires to tea. He's called Clarkie and he's quite nice, really. Just an ordinary Trabbershire man. He was very pleased to be asked but he said they're not allowed to eat with the people from the village. They all have to eat together up at the castle. So Granny sent him a pot of raspberry jam."

After tea they went to Billy's treehouse and looked out over the village. There were still men climbing the scaffolding, and the distant ringing of hammers.

"Don't they ever go to sleep?" wondered Drina.

"Will any of us, at this rate?" asked Billy.

It turned out to be a very good question.

# Chapter Eight

For the next three nights, building went on long after midnight and started early in the morning. The Twidings people, who were usually good-natured and easy-going, became grumpy from lack of sleep. The air was dry and gritty with the dust from brick and stone. Supplies of fish grew scarcer, and Drina gave all of hers to Jampot.

"It would have been a lot worse if you hadn't persuaded them to supply their own food," observed Granny. "At least we still have bread and suchlike, and we still have strawberries in the garden."

But the strawberries tasted of dust even after Drina had washed them. The fence kept the sun from cottage gardens. The air became dry and suffocating.

Nobody was allowed across the building site.

Poodle escaped once and ran across it, leaving a trail of pawprints in the cement before they chased him away, so Daffodil gave him a medal and a chocolate biscuit. He ate them both.

Even Granny Annie grew sad and listless. Her hand was a little better, so she tried to do her own hair, not altogether successfully – there were more hairpins than ever on the carpet – but she didn't seem to care. She was tired from lack of sleep and sunshine.

It turned out that the light at the Fiddlesteps' house was even worse than the light at Water's Edge Cottage. Gerbil had left an order for more green shirts, but the light was too poor to work by and the Fiddlesteps simple couldn't manage all that detailed sewing. At least, that was what they told Gerbil.

One afternoon everyone was so snappy for lack of sleep that Billy, Taffeta and Drina escaped to the treehouse and stayed there, with Jampot lying in the shade beneath it. If Drina stood on tiptoe she could just see the sparkle of sun far away on the lake.

"I want to look at something that hasn't been spoiled," she said. "I almost wish I hadn't come here, to see Twidings being taken over."

"You could go back," said Billy.

"No," she said, "I have to stay. I can't just walk out now."

"I'm glad you came," said Billy. "You think of things like Tough Stew, and you found the book of the Laws."

"But we can't make Gerbil keep them," she pointed out.

"He'll get his comeuppance at the Quarter Court," said Billy. "And we managed to warn all the girls not to marry him. If he can't marry anyone local he can't stay Lord of Lullwater."

"None of them would have married him anyway," said Drina. "Who would?"

"I wish he had married Granny Grind-Spirtle," said Taffeta, turning somersaults over a branch. "She's got a beard."

"Or Amazonia," said Drina. "She's the strong woman in the circus, and what's more, she's very tidy. She'd tuck him under her arm and put him away. In the lake, if—"

"Look, something's coming!" said Billy suddenly.

Drina turned. Billy was pointing to the path on the other side of the castle.

"Not another wagon!" said Drina.

But this was no builder's wagon. An elegant carriage pulled by two grey horses was trundling down the hill into the village. Green Shirts were running to the Village Green and knocking on cottage doors as they went, ushering everyone to the castle.

"They're busy," said Billy.

They climbed down and ran through the woods to the castle just in time to see the carriage roll to a stop in front of the gates. Granny was on her way, and Clarkie offered her his arm. Daffodil hurtled up, pink-faced and out of breath.

"I was fishing," she explained. "I'd barely got to the middle of the lake when Wendy-Jane appeared, waving

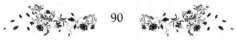

90

to come back. I hadn't even caught anything or got any reeds and I had to row all the way back and –" she stopped to gasp for breath, "– is that Gerbil in the carriage?"

"You never know, it might be," said Billy drily.

"The curtains are closed," Granny pointed out. "It could be anyone. How mysterious!"

"Silence!" roared Harry (or it might have been Gary). "Stand up for Gerbil, Lord of Lullwater!"

A Green Shirt opened the carriage door. Out stepped Gerbil in his grey suit and black velvet cloak.

"Greetings, my dear good people!" he called, and eyed them all with his head on one side. "Rejoice! Here I am, back among you!"

There was a silence, then the Green Shirts cheered.

"I said *rejoice!*" repeated Gerbil. "What is the matter with you? Am I speaking a foreign language?"

"We're delighted," said Granny politely.

Taffeta stifled a giggle. Gerbil glared.

"I have excellent news for all the people of Twidings-on-Lullwater," he said. "I have brought you the most wonderful gift!" He turned to the carriage. "My dear, don't be shy! Come and meet everyone!"

From inside the carriage came a high-pitched giggle. A thin leg appeared, with scarlet toenails and a high-heeled silver sandal. Stepping out and taking Gerbil's hand was a slender young woman in a red dress so clinging that Drina thought it must have been wound round her and pulled tight. Her hair hung in long blonde curls from a hairband the same bright red as her dress

91

and her gleaming nails. She carried a tiny silver bag, and twiddled her fingertips in a little wave at the crowd.

"Hello, everyone!" she said in a soft, breathy voice.

"Who on earth is she?" whispered Billy.

"She's got a voice like a marshmallow!" said Taffeta.

"Good heavens!" said Granny. "Can it be ... no, surely not!"

But a voice from the crowd shouted, "It's our little Twinkle! Hello, our Twinkle!"

Everyone turned to see who was speaking. Mrs Baggotty, her husband, and their sons were waving over the heads of the crowds.

"Over here, Twinkle!" they called, but were stopped by a look from Gerbil.

"My dear Twinkle is already known to many of you," he said. "She is a Twidings girl, born and bred. And she is soon to be the new Lady of Lullwater! We will be married before the next Quarter Court!"

"Twinkle!" cried Mrs Baggotty again.

Now that he had made his speech, Gerbil didn't attempt to keep her quiet. She pushed her way through the crowd, and Twinkle bent down to hug her. In those tall silver sandals, she reminded Drina of the circus stilt-walker.

"Twinkle Baggotty," sighed Granny sadly. "She's a real Twidings girl. She left the village years ago. Gerbil couldn't find anyone in the village who'd marry him, so he went looking elsewhere."

Taffeta had stopped laughing and peeped out from behind Granny. "She can't love him!" she said.

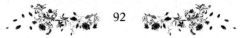

Granny shrugged. "Even Gerbil Cravat needs someone to love him," she said. "But I don't suppose she does. He's rich. He has a castle." She looked very tired and there was no laughter in her eyes.

"As you all know," went on Gerbil pompously, "I care deeply about this village and all you dear good people. My faithful team – Harry, Barry, Gary and Wendy-Jane – will soon tell me about all that has happened here in my absence. I'm looking forward so much to hearing what you've been up to."

He looked round the crowd and Drina shuddered. Was he looking directly at her or was she imagining it? She looked at Billy and knew that he felt the same.

"Let's go home, Granny," she said. "Jampot, come on."

She took Jampot's lead and turned away, then heard a sort of squeak from Twinkle Baggotty.

"Oh, my word!" gasped Twinkle. "What's that?"

Drina looked over her shoulder. Twinkle was pointing at Jampot.

"Jampot, sit," ordered Drina, and smoothed his mane to calm him. Jampot didn't really need calming, but she did.

Twinkle tottered over to them. "It isn't actually a lion, is it? Ooh – I think it is! A lion!"

"Yes – er – Miss Twinkle," said Drina.

"I heard that!" called Gerbil. "It's 'My Lady' to all of you. She may not be the Lady of Lullwater yet, but she soon will be, so you may as well practise it."

Jampot growled softly and pressed closer to Drina.

 93

Twinkle hesitated. "Does it bite?" she asked.

"No," said Daffodil. "He's old and he hasn't any teeth."

"Oh, then he's just a great big pussy cat!" exclaimed Twinkle, and bent down towards Jampot. "Hello, sweetie! Are you a great big old pussy cat then? You are, aren't you? Do you children go for rides on his back?"

"Certainly not!" said Drina. When she had been younger she had ridden Jampot – he had quite liked it, and used to lie down for her to get on – but she felt they were both too old for that now. "He's not that sort of lion."

Jampot's mouth stretched open in an immense yawn. Several people, including Twinkle, stepped back and Twinkle covered her nose and mouth. Her eyes widened. "Oh!" came her muffled voice through her hands. "That's – oh, that is. . ." She flapped the air and went on in a tight, choked voice. "Isn't he very well?"

"His breath isn't nice," admitted Drina. "It's just because he's getting old."

"Couldn't you do anything about it?" purred Twinkle. "Feed him peppermints or rose petals? He's such a darling!"

"My dear," interrupted Gerbil, "we must talk to Mr Goodenough about our wedding. Let's not keep the common people from their work. They have such busy little lives, and I'm sure they want to get together and make plans to celebrate our marriage." He smiled, and a small child nearby began to wail. "They will be

94

planning music, parties and dancing, I'm sure. Off you go, my people."

Granny Annie pulled her shawl tightly round her and rubbed her arms. "I'm cold," she said. "Let's go home, Drina."

"Of course it's cold," muttered Uncle Tam Fiddlestep. "They've built that fence even higher. That's even more light blotted out."

Drina lay awake that night. The worry and the noise from the building site – neither seemed to stop. She wriggled against the wall so that there was room for Jampot on the bed beside her and he lay awake too, knowing Drina was unhappy.

For the first time since coming to Twidings, Drina missed her family. Between them, Ma, Pa, Sapphire and Spangle would have sorted out Gerbil Cravat. Amazonia certainly would. Magnificent Merlin the Escapologist was so good at getting out of locked cages, surely he could have put Gerbil into one? It had been fun playing tricks on Gerbil, warning all the girls not to marry him and making Tough Stew. But it wasn't fun any more. How would it all end?

Drina's thoughts flew round her head until at last, Jampot's warmth helped her drift off to sleep.

She was woken by a furious banging on the door, and ran downstairs to open it. Taffeta fell into her arms. Her hair was wild and she sobbed so loudly, Drina could hardly understand a word.

"They – they – Mum!" she sobbed. "Dad! Those men!"

"What men?" asked Drina urgently. "Shh, Taffy. Try to tell me."

Jampot padded lightly down the stairs and ran to her side. Taffeta let go of Drina, threw herself at Jampot, and wept into his mane.

Finally she dried her eyes on the back of her hand.

"They came for Mum and Dad," she gulped. "Gary and some of the Green Shirts. They took them to the castle. Mum and Dad didn't want to go, but Gary said they had to. It was Gerbil's orders! Satin and Linen and the boys said they'd all go, but Gary said no, just Mum and Dad!"

"Who does that man think he is?" came Granny's voice from the top of the stairs. She stood on the landing in her dressing gown, holding her toothbrush like a weapon. "He can't do that! Taffeta, help me to get dressed, then send for Billy! Drina, have an idea! We need to sort this out!"

# Chapter Nine

Drina pulled on her clothes, left Granny and Taffeta to look after each other and ran to the castle with Jampot keeping pace at her side. She arrived, out of breath, to find Gary and Harry guarding the gate, and realized that she didn't know what to say or how to say it.

"I need to see Ger . . . the Lord of Lullwater," she said. "I mean, I need to see the Fiddlesteps. Please."

"No, you don't," said Gary (or it might have been Harry). "You need to go home and do something useful."

"I would like to see them," said Drina politely. "Please take a message to Mr Cravat."

"You asked a question, you got an answer," said Gary or Harry. "It's 'no', and it's the only one you're getting. You can stand here all day and we'll still say 'no'."

Drina remembered a trick that the circus clowns used to play. "So," she said, "if I stand here all day and keep asking, you'll still say. . ."

"No," they both said together.

"Then," said Drina, "do you mind if I see the Lord of Lullwater?"

Gary (or it might have been Barry) and Harry opened their mouths to speak, shut them again, and looked at each other.

"Don't try to be—" began Gary, as the doors opened suddenly to let out a team of Green Shirts.

Jampot crouched and growled. From somewhere in the castle, Twinkle's light, marshmallow voice called out, "Is that the girl with the darling lion? Let her in! Let them both in!"

"Excuse me, My Lady," said Gary or Barry, "but our orders are—"

"But nothing," said Twinkle and came click-clicking to the door in shoes with heels like knitting needles. She was wearing a tight white dress and clutching her sparkly silver bag. "Hello, sweetie! What's your name?"

"Drina Snapdragon," said Drina.

"Oh, you're dear old Annie's granddaughter!" said Twinkle. "Come in, darling! Boys, let her in or I'll speak to Gerbil about you. Bring your lion."

Drina looked past her at the wide grey hall of the castle. It was plain, grim and forbidding with an unlit fire in the grate and brackets on the walls for candles, which at this time of day were unlit. Jampot pressed

closer to Drina, and she stroked his head to reassure both of them.

"Are you looking at the castle?" asked Twinkle. "This bit's the Great Hall and all the other rooms and little corridors and staircases lead from it. It's awfully dull, isn't it, but when it's finished it'll be a fairytale palace! In you come, and we'll have a chat over some lovely cold lemonade."

"Thank you, but I came to see my aunt and uncle," said Drina, still on the doorstep. "The Fiddlesteps."

"What a simply lovely idea!" cried Twinkle with a lift of her shoulders as if seeing the Fiddlesteps was the most exciting thing anybody had ever heard of. "In you come!"

Drina stepped into the hall and couldn't help a shudder. Jampot paced so closely beside her that she could feel his coat against her legs.

Jampot would rather be anywhere but this. But he had Drina to look after.

"Are you cold, darling?" asked Twinkle. "Isn't it amazing how cold it is in here, and when it's so sunny outside! It'll soon be cosy. I want to put a fish tank under the floor with sparkly lights so that you can come in and see all the little fishes swimming about and the pretty lights. I want everything to be beautiful. That's why we invited the Fiddlesteps."

"Invited?" repeated Drina. She could feel Gary and Harry watching her with nasty smiles on their faces. Jampot's growl was embarrassingly loud.

"Jampot, quiet," she said. Jampot, who always

obeyed her, went on growling, but more softly. "Please, Miss Twinkle – My Lady – I heard that the Fiddlesteps were brought here by Green Shirt people early this morning whether they wanted to come or not. The family are very upset."

"Oh, were the boys naughty, getting them up so early?" asked Twinkle, frowning prettily. "I hope they weren't rough. I'll speak to them about that, we can't have people upset. Harry, Larry, Furry – whatever your names are – shut the doors! Now, Drina, let's find the Fiddlesteps! Mrs Fiddlestep is your auntie, isn't she?"

In spite of Twinkle's sweet, silly manner Drina almost expected to find the Fiddlesteps in a dungeon with water running down the walls. But Twinkle showed her into a pleasant, white-painted room with a long table and a fire in the grate. At the table, Aunt Jemima and Uncle Tam were studying paper patterns and snippets of cloth. They looked up when Drina came in. There was something about Aunt Jemima's expression – half welcome and half fear – that worried Drina.

"Mr and Mrs Fiddlestep are helping me with some designs," said Twinkle happily. "Dear Gerbil wanted them to make more green shirts for our helpers, but they sort of didn't want to, so the Greenies brought them up here to talk to him. Anyway, I was ever so thrilled to see them, because I want our people to have proper uniforms instead of silly old boring green shirts. Mr and Mrs Fiddlestep are helping me choose patterns and some really gorgeous fabrics!" She put her head round the door and called to someone. "Thingy –

100

whatever your name is, you in the green – yes, you – bring in a pot of tea and those nice biscuits I brought from Carillon, and two glasses of lemonade with lots of fizz and little cherries on sticks."

Twinkle poured tea and handed round biscuits, but Aunt Jemima and Uncle Tam still looked uneasy. Lemonade arrived, foaming over the tops of the glasses, with cherries bobbing on top like ducks in a bath. Twinkle sat down at the table beside Aunt Jemima and offered Drina a chair.

"Now, Drina," she said, "I thought for the boys we could maybe have emerald green with white stripes, and white trousers, and silver cufflinks for the important ones like the Barry-Harry whatever they are. And pink with silver trim for the girls. What do you think? If you worked for us, would you rather have pink, and maybe a puff sleeve, or something really dramatic like purple and silver?"

"I don't know and I don't mind," said Drina. Jampot stood up and growled more loudly as the door opened.

"Gerbil, darling!" cried Twinkle. She jumped up and gave him a tiny peck of a kiss, which he ignored. Jampot sat on Drina's foot, which she liked.

"I see young Andrina has joined us," he said smoothly, and without smiling. "What do you think of Miss Baggotty's idea?"

"I don't want to work for you and I don't care about the uniforms," she said.

Gerbil's eyebrows drew closer together and he looked puzzled.

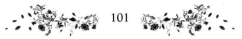 101

"Oh, *that* idea!" trilled Twinkle. "We haven't talked about *that* yet. Drina came up here to see her auntie and uncle, didn't you, sweetie?"

"How pleasant," said Gerbil, "and how convenient. It saves me the trouble of sending for you. Mr and Mrs Fiddlestep, I had hoped to enjoy your company a little longer, but for now, would you like to go home to your family and see what they think about the new uniforms? When the hotels are built the whole village will work for me, and I want them to look smart. I will send for you again."

Aunt Jemima still looked anxious. "Will you be all right here, Drina?" she asked.

"Of course!" said Drina brightly, because she wanted the Fiddlesteps to be safely out of Gerbil's way. Taffeta would be a lot happier if they were back home. She reached down to curl her fingers in Jampot's mane and he turned his head to look up into her face and lick her wrist. Aunt Jemima cast a last glance at her from the doorway.

"Andrina, the future Lady of Lullwater, has a suggestion for you," said Gerbil. "Twinkle, my dear, would you like to explain?"

Twinkle folded her hands. She leaned forward and spoke to Drina as if she were a very small child.

"I'm glad you've brought your lion," she said. "You take ever such good care of him, don't you?"

While Drina wondered how she was supposed to answer such a stupid question, Twinkle went on, "He's ever so well behaved. What do you call him?"

 102

"Jampot," said Drina, and didn't explain why.

Twinkle gave a twitter of laughter. "How funny! Shouldn't he have a big, liony name, like Leo or King?"

Drina shrugged.

"And is he very tame?" asked Twinkle.

Drina hesitated. If she said "yes", they would think he couldn't protect her. If she said "no", Gerbil might have him put into a cage as a wild animal.

"It depends on what you mean by 'tame'," she said cautiously.

"He's been as good as gold today," said Twinkle. "He does have a problem with his smelly breath, but we could do something about that."

*We?* Cold ran down Drina's spine and along her arms so that the hairs stood up.

"A change to his diet would do it, I'm sure," went on Twinkle. "If we give him lots of rose water to drink he'll smell as sweet as a bouquet."

"I don't know what you mean," said Drina. But she was afraid that she did.

"It's very simple," said Gerbil. "The future Lady of Lullwater is making a very generous offer to buy the lion."

Something seemed to spin in Drina's head. Her ears were ringing. "He's not for sale," she said, and her voice sounded far away.

"Then I'll *take* him," said Gerbil.

Drina shrieked. She couldn't help it. Even Twinkle looked shocked.

The growl in Jampot's throat grew deep and loud, and Drina hugged him tightly.

"You can't!" cried Drina. "The Quarter Court—"

"Oh, that," said Gerbil. "I'm sure I can persuade the judge to see reason. Everyone does, eventually. Now listen while the future Lady of Lullwater explains it to you."

Twinkle still looked surprised. She gave herself a little shake, then leaned towards Drina again.

"You see, darling," she said, "ever since I saw your Jampot, I've been thinking he's so adorable, I just *have* to have one."

"Oh," said Drina with relief. "Do you mean any lion? I might be able to find you another rescued circus lion and teach you how to look after it. I don't know about any just now, but my family might. You'd have to be—"

"But this one is so very special, isn't he?" purred Twinkle. "It would simply have to be dear Jampot. He's so gorgeous, and I promise you, Drina, I'd take the very best care of him. You could tell me all about what he likes to eat and where he'd like to sleep and all about his walkies and playtimes. He'd be the castle lion; he'd be ever so important. You see, Drina darling, I'm sure your Granny's cottage is ever so sweet and dinky and cosy but a castle is much better for a lion, isn't it? And if you go back home to your circus, he won't have to live in a nasty wagon, he can stay here with me in my fairytale palace. We can make his breath smell sweet—"

"And if that doesn't work we can put him in a muzzle," said Gerbil.

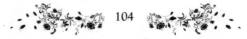

"No!" screamed Drina.

"Oh, it won't come to that!" protested Twinkle. "If he had a muzzle we couldn't hear his big, brave roar, could we?"

"He doesn't roar," said Drina.

"No roar?" said Twinkle. "We'll teach him to do a big, brave roar. Drina, dear, I do understand. I know he means ever so much to you, so let's see what we can arrange. I wonder what you'd like?"

*Twinkle isn't a bad person,* Drina told herself. *Just silly. I have to make her understand.*

"He's my best friend," she said. "He loves me. I can't sell him."

"That's strange," remarked Gerbil. "I thought the Fiddlestep children were your best friends. And your grandmother."

Drina heard the threat in his voice and wished she was somewhere else.

"Of course they are!" cried Twinkle. "Drina, when Jampot comes to live here you can see him every day. We can't have him pining for you, can we? You can come to play whenever you like! So what shall we arrange? What about a nicer house for your granny?"

"She loves her cottage," said Drina.

"Let me see then," said Twinkle, "because I do understand, I really do. Of course no money would be enough... What about free lake permits for you and your granny and all your Fiddlestep chums for ever and ever? And what about a pony? Would you like a pony?"

Drina shuffled a little closer to Twinkle before speaking. She didn't want Gerbil to hear. Jampot shuffled too.

"Please, Twinkle – I mean, Miss Baggotty," said Drina quietly. "I was very little when I first met Jampot, but I can still remember it. We got him from a circus where they'd worked him almost to death. They used to feed him rubbishy food. He was never groomed or washed and he slept on damp, dirty straw, so he was ill and thin and they were going to shoot him. They only agreed to let us have him if we didn't tell anyone where we got him from. I was tiny, but I wanted to be the one who looked after him. I carried water and food to him. I brushed him with my own little hairbrush. When we got him he had fleas and ticks and all sorts and I combed and combed."

"Eeuw, how nasty!" squeaked Twinkle.

"He hasn't got them now," added Drina, "but what I mean is, I've looked after him all my life. I made him well. We go everywhere together. He'll die if I'm not there."

"Then you can come to see him!" said Twinkle sweetly. "In fact, I think I could persuade darling Gerbil to build you a little room in the castle so you can live here with him."

Drina could almost have agreed to this, but it would mean moving into the castle, away from her granny and her friends, and Gerbil would always be about.

"Oh, yes," said Gerbil without smiling. "She can certainly have a room in the castle."

Under Drina's hand, Jampot's muscles tensed.

She looked Gerbil in the eyes. "Do you mean a dungeon?" she asked.

"Don't be silly!" laughed Twinkle.

"Dear girl," said Gerbil, "there are no dungeons here."

"No, there really aren't," agreed Twinkle.

"Come with me, Drina," said Gerbil.

Drina hesitated. Jampot put his paw very firmly over her foot. Then a commotion of shouting erupted from the door, and everyone turned. One of the voices was Billy's. Drina and Jampot ran to the sound.

"Billy!" she called. He was struggling against two Green Shirts who held him firmly by the arms.

"Where's Dri— Oh, there you are," said Billy. "Are you all right?" Then he saw Gerbil, and didn't wait for an answer. "First you take Mum and Dad, and now Drina!"

"Your parents have gone home," said Gerbil. "Really, what a fuss! They were invited to the castle for a meeting with the future Lady of Lullwater. The Green Shirts even went to call for them. But I did also want to see you, Billy. I would like you two cousins to come with me, please. Bring the lion."

Drina caught Billy's eye and he nodded. There were two of them and a lion, after all. They followed Gerbil down the corridor to a black door with "Sitting Room" painted on it.

"Can't be that bad," whispered Billy. "It's a sitting room."

A green-shirted man opened the door and they found themselves in a small room containing nothing but a black table with a grey chair behind it. The walls were painted not exactly black but a very dark grey, rather like black but less exciting. There was one tiny window, high up, so even on a summer day the room was dark and chilly.

"Do sit down," said Gerbil, and seated himself in the only chair with the Green Shirt standing behind him like a bodyguard. "Sit on the floor. Or stand. I don't care. It's time you understood the future of this village, as you seem to love it so much."

Drina and Billy sat down with Jampot between them. Drina couldn't exactly hold Jampot's hand, so she put her hand over his paw.

"For too long," said Gerbil, "this village has been wasted. A lake, fish, woods, cottages, hard-working people, a castle and nobody in it. All this time you had no proper Lord of the Manor – only old Thumping-Jolly, who let you all do what you liked. Where's the Lording in that? And there are people like me – very few – who are perfectly cut out to be Lords of Manors, running villages, making money, building houses, and making the rules. So here I am! A proper Lord of the Manor. You should all be grateful."

"It's not meant to be like that," said Drina. "The Lord of the Manor has duties to the people. It's in *The Lullwater Laws*. The Lord of Lullwater has to be a fair and just lord—"

"No, he doesn't," snapped Gerbil. "I know what

the Laws say, and I intend to change them. A Lord of the Manor should get his own way. I'm spending my money on your village; I can expect you all to do as you're told."

Drina hoped she didn't look as frightened as she felt. She wished Jampot had proper teeth.

"What's the matter?" continued Gerbil. "Do you think I'm going to turn you out of your homes or make you all into slaves, or send my Green Shirts to beat you up? My solution is much simpler than that. The best ideas are simple, and my ideas are the best. I will let you into the secret of how I will control this village. My young Snapdragon, my young Fiddlestep, think of my building site by the lake. What does it take away from you?"

"The lake," said Billy promptly.

"Yes, and. . .?"

"The shore," said Drina.

"Reeds and fish," offered Billy.

"The view," said Drina.

"Getting closer," said Gerbil. "Come on, you small and wretched shreds of disgrace, what else?"

Drina realized what he meant. "The sunlight," she said.

"Say that again," ordered Gerbil.

"The sunlight," repeated Drina.

"Just so," said Gerbil. "I am taking away the sunlight. Did you know that people need sunlight in order to live? Already my buildings are keeping the sun from the houses, the streets, the Village Green – people are

getting miserable, and I've only just started."

"But what about your visitors?" asked Billy. "They'll want sunshine."

"Oh, they'll get plenty, don't worry," sneered Gerbil. "The sun will simply pour into those buildings, but it won't reach the village. Your houses will be in shadow and you won't be able to keep them warm. Your gardens will wither for want of light. You will be cold, summer and winter. You won't be able to grow food. You won't be able to fish without a permit – not that there will be many fish; the guests at the hotel will have caught them. This is how I intend to break the spirits of you termites, you toadstools, you Twiders. I will stand between you and the sun."

"But you don't own the sunshine," said Drina.

"Who does?" asked Gerbil. "You?"

"No," she said. "Nobody does. It's there for everyone."

"So is misery!" snapped Gerbil. "And you need to know about it! My dear Twinkle Baggotty, the future Lady of Lullwater, said that we don't have dungeons. She was right. We have a sitting room. I am the Lord of Lullwater and anyone who upsets me will be put in this room, or one very like it, and given nothing but bread and water. Oh, and a chamber pot. Nothing else. No company, no visitors, no sound, no books, no games, no anything. Alone in a grey room without sunshine."

"Sounds like a dungeon to me," said Billy, but Gerbil ignored him.

"It wouldn't be very nice, would it?" said Gerbil.

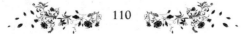

"You wouldn't like it if I kept you in one of these rooms, would you, Andrina? Perhaps you should think again about what the future Lady of Lullwater requires. That lion will be hers. You will get a generous reward and the chance to see him whenever the Lady of Lullwater says you may. You can have your own room in the castle, much nicer than this one. If you are difficult, Andrina, if you refuse to let the future Lady of Lullwater have what would make her so happy, you will stay as my sitting-room guest."

Drina and Billy darted to the door. It was locked. The growl in Jampot's throat grew louder and deeper.

"Jampot, quiet!" whispered Drina. She was afraid of what Gerbil might do to a lion who threatened him.

But Gerbil was talking to Billy.

"Billy," he was saying, "I was hoping you'd come to call. I'd been told that you had built a treehouse in the wood, so I made it my business to take a look at it."

"That's my house!" shouted Billy.

"That's *my* tree," said Gerbil smoothly, "and I'm most impressed by what you've built in it. Here is what I suggest... Visitors to the village might like to stay in treehouses. Not yours, of course; not a ramshackle hut like that. They'd want luxury dwellings with hot and cold running water, carpets and curtains. I would like you to build treehouses for me."

"I'd rather not, Lord Cravat," said Billy as politely as he could.

Gerbil leaned back in his chair. "I see," he said. "You do like your treehouse, don't you, Billy?" he said.

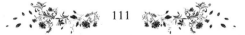 111

"You wouldn't like it to fall down?"

"You mean, if I don't help you, you'll destroy my house?" said Billy.

"I didn't say that, did I?" said Gerbil with an unpleasant smile. "Billy, Andrina, think seriously about this. Andrina, allow your lion to receive the loving care of the future Lady of Lullwater. Billy, I hope you will help me. Because," he pressed his fingertips together, "I'm thinking about your grandmother and your sweet little sister."

"Leave Taffeta alone!" shouted Billy.

"And Granny!" said Drina, but Gerbil continued as if they hadn't spoken.

"They wouldn't like it in the grey sitting room all summer without sunshine, would they?" said Gerbil. "So perhaps you will both do as I say."

# Chapter Ten

Drina leaned against Jampot, hearing the strong, steady beat of his heart. It helped her to think.

"You're an evil man," she said. "I can't stop you taking Jampot, but if any harm comes to him I will make sure the judge sends you to a prison in a hole in the ground with cockroaches. For ever."

"Now, let me see," said Gerbil, "I've managed to take over this village without too much difficulty. I think my Green Shirts and I can cope with a Quarter Court judge. I'll call Gary to take the lion to the future Lady of Lullwater."

That wasn't in Drina's plan. "He won't go with just anyone," she said. "If he isn't handled by somebody he knows, he could get very difficult."

"He'll get distressed," put in Billy.

"And when he's distressed he starts destroying things," said Drina, trying to stay calm as she made this up. "And there's something else that Tw . . . the Future Lady of Lullwater needs to know. As I said before, when he first came to us he had fleas and ticks and things."

Gerbil's moustache twitched. He pushed his chair back.

"He doesn't have them now," she said, "not exactly. But he has to have his medicinal bath with herbs and Granny's special soap once a month, and he's due for one now. If he doesn't have that his skin gets flaky and sore, and. . ."

"And the scabs drop off everywhere," offered Billy.

". . .and there are still insect eggs under his skin and if he doesn't get his special bath they hatch and come wriggling out. . ."

"And they don't just bite him, they bite *people*," said Billy. "And the bites get itchy and red. . ."

"So he can't come until he's had his bath," explained Drina. "It takes hours to get him washed and dried."

"Bath him here," ordered Gerbil. "The Green Shirts will fetch everything you need."

"I'm sorry, but that won't work," said Drina. "He gets upset enough having it done at Granny's house. I don't know what he'd do in a strange place. It's very hard getting a lion into a bath when he doesn't want to go."

"And he moults," added Billy. "Lots. Everywhere."

"I see," said Gerbil. From his face, Drina couldn't tell whether he believed them or not. "Billy, the lion

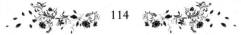

appears to be happy in your company. Take him to your grandmother's house and give him his bath with whatever scrawny herbs her garden can provide and whatever obnoxious soaps she uses and bring him back by nine o'clock tomorrow morning. Andrina, you will stay here. When the lion is returned, you may go."

"That's not fair!" shouted Billy. "That's keeping her as a hostage!"

"Oh, dear, no," said Gerbil. "She will be a visitor in the castle. What a lucky girl! The sooner you go, Billy, the sooner you can come back. I do look forward to working on treehouses with you."

"Just go," said Drina quickly. At least Billy would be safe. "Go and make sure that he has a really good bath." She searched for the right words and looked Billy in the eyes. "So everything gets washed right away."

"I can do that," said Billy.

"Now, Jampot," she said, kneeling in front of him. He raised a paw and she took it in both her hands, loving the velvety warmth of it. His gaze was strong and steady, trusting her so completely that it was almost unbearable. "Go with Billy. Be a good lion." She squeezed her eyes shut and hugged him tightly. "Good lion," she whispered in his ear. "Be good for Granny." If she kept repeating their names, he might go without feeling too puzzled about why she wasn't going with him. "Billy, Taffeta, Granny Annie."

She raised her head from the familiar warm smell of his mane and looked up at Billy. It was all she could do

to keep her face from crumpling into tears.

"Make him think it's all right," was all she could say.

Billy patted his leg as if Jampot were a dog. "Come on then, Jampot!" he called. "Let's have a run! Find Taffeta!"

Drina pressed her face into her hands until the sound of Billy's running feet had faded away. Soon his cry of, "Come on then, Jampot! Good lion!" carried to her from outside. They were safe for now.

She looked up to see Gerbil standing between her and the door.

"That was entertaining," he said. "Now, my dear, the sitting room is all yours until tomorrow morning. Goodbye."

Drina dashed to the door, but he was too quick. The door closed behind him and she heard the click of a key turning in the lock.

And again. Again. There were three locks.

She threw herself at the door, ready to bang at it and scream, then decided that it wouldn't do any good. For the same reason she made up her mind not to feel sorry for herself or cry. She took a few deep breaths and walked slowly round the grey room, considering. She'd just have to do her thinking without Jampot.

As Gerbil had said, there was a grey chamber pot behind a grey screen. There was the chair Gerbil had been sitting on and the table. Drina opened the drawers but they were empty except for a pencil with no point and a dead fly. She dragged the chair against the wall

 116

and stood on it, but the small, high window was still too far up for her to see anything. She tried standing on the desk, which didn't help much, so, having grown up in a circus, she balanced the chair on the desk and climbed on top of that.

She wished she could see the lake, the shore and Granny Annie's house, but once she had climbed up she realized that this room was at the back of the castle, facing the wooded hillside, and there wasn't much to see at all. Trees nestled up against the wall, and through them she could just glimpse the train chugging its way to Carillon.

She climbed carefully down and considered how to escape. The window was out of reach and too small for her to climb through. She could throw things at it – the pencil and the chamber pot perhaps – but it wouldn't draw any attention, not on that side of the castle. What did she have? A desk, a chair, a chamber pot, a broken pencil and a dead fly. The clothes she stood up in – dungarees, a shirt and sandals. What else?

She had everything that was in her head, all the knowledge, stories and songs she had learnt, her talents, her thinking and her cleverness. She had her loving, her wisdom and her strength. She had what was in her mind and in her heart.

Oh, and in her pockets.

She swiftly emptied them. They contained a pencil (with a point), a dog-eared notebook, some shells, a few bits of twide she'd been fidgeting with and some of Granny Annie's dropped hairpins. She stared down

at those hairpins and stroked them with a fingertip the way you might stroke a particularly tiny kitten. But the time to use them was not yet. She should wait until dark.

To keep herself from going mad with boredom she sang every song she knew, then told herself every story she knew and made up a few more of her own. When somebody brought her bread and water she glanced round the door to see where the guards were posted, but she couldn't get a good look. She left some water in the cup in case she needed it later.

The day seemed to be everlasting. She took the drawer out of the desk and amused herself by flipping shells into it. Then she thought she'd better learn to find her way in the dark, so she walked round the room with her eyes shut, running her fingers along the walls and counting until she knew how many steps it took her to cross the room, and how to reach the door from the desk. Then she grew cold, and banged at the door. Nothing happened, so she kicked it and screamed until somebody opened it, just a crack.

"I need a blanket," she said firmly. "If I don't have one I might freeze to death and then you'd all be arrested for murder."

Presently the blanket was pushed through the door and Drina heard Twinkle say something like, "Oh, is it the Trabby-wabby men's turn now?" before the door was shut and locked again. If this bit of Twinkle-talk meant that the Trabbershire men were coming on duty it could be a good thing. Better than the Green Shirts.

She wondered about Jampot. If Billy had understood what she meant about "a proper bath" so that everything would be "washed away", he'd be hiding Jampot away somewhere that Gerbil's men would never find him. It would be good to make Granny and Taffeta and the Fiddlesteps disappear too, before Gerbil could take them and lock them in his grey room. But it would be hard enough to hide a lion, let alone a whole family.

When it was so dark that Drina could see nothing at all she slipped her hand into her pocket for the hairpins. Merlin the Magnificent had taught her to open locks, which was a useful skill if anyone lost the key to a wagon or a costume basket. That sort of thing happened a lot in the circus, so Drina was well practised.

The top lock looked hardest, being well out of her reach. Even standing on the chair with the desk drawer upside down on top of it she had to stretch. Then she had the idea of folding up the blanket and adding it to the heap, which made it higher but wobbly. She pressed at the levers with the hair pin. Nothing moved. She turned hot and cold with anxiety. Her hand shook.

"Calm down," she told herself. "Try again. Try differently."

After some deep breaths, a lot of failure and a little panic, she felt the lock move. *Click*. By daylight the bottom lock had looked tricky so she tackled that one next, lying on the floor. It turned as smoothly as Granny Annie's spinning wheel.

*Yes!* Drina held up the hairpin and bowed to the

imaginary circus audience cheering and clapping for her. There was only one lock still to open and she ran her fingers across the door until she found the big, solid keyhole and slipped the hairpin into it.

Nothing happened. She tried again. The levers felt stiff and resisted her. *Do it for Granny Annie,* she told herself. This time, the hairpin snapped. She tried another, her heart beating more quickly. When her hand started hurting she sat on the floor to think.

Even if she did get the door open, she still had to get past however many guards were on the doors, and out of the castle. She couldn't depend on all of them being Trabbershire men, and even if they were, they might not be pleasant and reasonable like Clarkie. She'd have to distract their attention. What did she have for that? Dead fly, pencils, paper, shells, a bit of twide and a cup of water.

She took the twide from her pocket and dropped it into the water; wet twide would probably be better than dry twide for making guards fall over. She put the shells in the water too, for the same reason, then rubbed her aching hand. Time for another try at the lock. She held the hairpin close to her lips.

"Do this for me," she whispered, and kissed it. "Do it for Granny Annie."

She slipped into the lock, felt for the levers and stopped. Outside, there were running footsteps, then a sound of crying that made Drina gasp and her heart beat harder, because it was Taffeta, somewhere near, crying loudly and desperately.

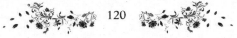

Fury rose up in her and she leapt to her feet, hurled herself at the door and turned the hairpin at the same time. The door gave way so suddenly that she stumbled against the opposite wall. She picked herself up and ran towards the glowing light of candles in the Great Hall.

For a moment, Drina couldn't believe her luck. There were no guards anywhere. Then she saw someone coming: a cloaked and hooded figure, all in black, was running towards her. She backed away, hoping for a corridor, a stairway, anywhere that wouldn't lead her back to the grey room...

"Shh!" The figure lifted a black-gloved finger to its lips. "Drina, it's me!"

"Daffodil!" whispered Drina.

Daffodil lifted the hood and peered out from underneath it. She grabbed Drina's wrist and pulled her into a corner. "Billy told us what happened," she said, softly and quickly. "Daddy said he knew we still had a set of castle keys somewhere if he could only remember where he'd put it and he said he hoped Gerbil hadn't changed the locks yet, and we looked everywhere because he thought they were in—"

"That's wonderful, Daffodil," said Drina. "You're amazing. But Taffeta's crying! What happened?"

"We found them in Poodle's bed." said Daffodil. "Oh, you mean Taffy? She's fine. She's good at crying, isn't she? It's part of the plan. I dressed up in black so nobody would see me, and I've got a candlehat under here. Don't worry, the candles are out – I blew them out when we got near the castle. Then Taffy did the crying so that the guards would run to find out what was the matter and I used my keys to get in and now we have to get out. I mean, get you out." She took a candle from a bracket on the wall and handed it to Drina.

"Where's Taffeta now?" asked Drina.

"Don't worry about her," Daffodil told her. "She's clever. She'll be telling some guard that she's lost in the night and hurt her poor little foot, and in no time they'll be patting her hand and taking her home. But it's too dangerous to go out the way I came in. Taffeta can't handle all the guards at once. I locked the doors after me so nobody can find them open and get suspicious."

"Do you know another way?" asked Drina.

"Back kitchens," whispered Daffodil promptly, leading the way. "The castle used to be ours, so Dad sort of knows it pretty well. There's a side door – um – over there, and we might be able to get out that way. If not, we can always try windows."

"There'll be guards all round the castle," Drina warned her. "We might have to run."

"Or we can talk our way out," said Daffodil cheerfully. "I'm good at talking."

They had reached the end of the passageway and Daffodil tried the door to the back kitchens. It was locked and none of the keys fitted it.

"We could run hard at it," said Daffodil.

"It's all right," said Drina. "I can do locks." She still had the last hairpin, and at the first turn the door swung open. Two guards stood on the other side.

"Told you," said one to the other. "Told you there was

a noise. One minute there's a kid crying outside then I could have sworn I heard something in the Great Hall. It's turning into an ogging busy night, this. What are you two doing here?"

At that moment, and without Jampot, Drina had one of her best ideas ever. She stepped very gently on Daffodil's toe to prompt her to be quiet. Then she held up the candle in front of her as far from Daffodil as possible.

"Two?" she said. "What do you mean?" She looked over her shoulder past Daffodil. "I can't see anyone."

"There," said one of the men, but already he sounded uncertain. "There, in the black."

Drina looked again, then widened her eyes and lowered her voice. "Are you *sure* you can see someone?"

"There," he said. His hand was shaking as he pointed. "There, just behind you."

Drina turned to the other man. "Did you see anyone?" she asked.

"I thought I..." he began. "Yes. Yes. There, in the black, just there."

Drina gasped, bit her lip, and hoped Daffodil wouldn't do anything silly like waving her arms and making ghost noises. She raised her hand.

"Spirit of the night, be silent!" she ordered, and added, "And stay silent."

She turned back to the men. "I've never seen it," she said, "but everyone knows there's an ootie in the castle. They call it ... no, I'd better not tell you what they call it because it doesn't like to be named. Or stared at. It might get angry."

Behind her, from somewhere in the castle, she could hear voices. She was fairly sure that one of them was Harry, or it might have been Barry.

"What do you mean, you can't find anything?" he was saying. "You haven't looked properly. I heard something in the Great Hall!"

"Don't look at it!" said Drina. "Mr Murgatroyd looked at it and died. And Mr Day saw it and the next day he fell out of the train."

The men were staring at the sky now, to make it quite clear they weren't looking at the ootie. Drina looked over her shoulder again, not to pretend that she couldn't see Daffodil, but to see if any Green Shirts were coming.

"I might be able to lead it away," she said. "I'll try."

"Search everywhere!" cried Harry.

"Is the ootie angry with us?" asked one of the men.

"Not *yet*," said Drina. "I'll do what I can." She turned back to Daffodil. "Spirit of the night, I am a Daughter of Twidings. Let me lead you from this place."

Daffodil bowed her head and followed Drina out of the castle as the men gazed at the stars. By the light of Drina's candle they picked their way over stones and grass, holding hands to keep their balance.

"Ouch!" muttered Drina as she turned her foot on a sharp stone. When she'd lived with the circus there was always a fire-juggler happy to help her find her way in the dark.

From the castle came a crash.

"Ow!" yelled Harry. "Why's that floor wet! And

where's that girl?"

"What's happening?" asked Daffodil.

"He fell over on some wet twide," said Drina. "Time to run!"

She caught a glimpse of Taffeta's patchwork jacket as somebody grabbed her and pulled her to the ground.

# Chapter Eleven

With a thud and a squeak, Daffodil fell over Drina.

"Drina!" she whispered. "They've got Taffy! Do the ootie thing again!"

"It's all right!" whispered Taffeta, running towards them across the grass. "It's Clarkie and he's on our side. But we have to get away."

Drina's candle had gone out as she fell. She reached for it. "Anyone got matches?" she asked.

"No light!" said Taffeta. "We mustn't be noticed. Granny's left a light in her window to help us."

"I'll leave you young ladies to look after yourselves," said Clarkie. "I've had enough of Mr Cravat and I'm not the only one. I'll go to the castle and say I saw you running off t'other way towards the Carillon road. Send my good wishes to Mrs Snapdragon."

126

"We will, and thank you," whispered Drina. There was a surprised "Ooh!" as Taffeta flung her arms round Clarkie's neck and kissed him. Then Drina, Taffeta and Daffodil were holding hands and stumbling down the hillside until the door of Granny's cottage was opened for them.

Warmth and light rushed in on Drina and made her blink, then Granny was holding her in a one-armed hug and Jampot was putting up his paws and licking her face with joy. But the smell and the feel of him had changed, and when Drina looked down at him she caught her breath and dropped to her knees.

"What happened?" she said. "You beauty, what happened to you?"

Jampot's transformation was breathtaking. His coat was lighter than before, and gleamed. His mane was wave on wave of gold and felt silky under her hands, and the paw he offered her was perfectly smooth. He looked up at her and she thought his eyes were laughing.

"What have you done with him?" she asked, and hugged him. "He's..." She sat back on her heels. "He's three shades lighter, for a start."

"Let's begin at the beginning," said Granny. "Are you hungry?"

"*I* am," said Taffeta.

Granny brought in soup and bread and gooseberry pie, and to Drina it tasted like the best food she'd ever eaten. Between mouthfuls, Billy explained what had been happening.

 127

"When I got back from the castle, Daffodil came to see what was going on, and she said she'd help," he began.

"Yes, and we decided we needed to get you and Jampot out of the village," interrupted Daffodil, "so I went to Nithering Day and explained, and he said he could run the Day Train specially for you except it wouldn't be in the day so it would be the Night Train but that doesn't matter because—"

"Have some more bread, Daffodil dear," said Granny. "Yes, Drina, you and Jampot aren't safe here any longer. We'll get you out of the village at sunrise."

"What about the rest of you?" asked Drina. "Gerbil Cravat might put any of you in his grey room!" She told them what Gerbil had said to her. "He wants to deprive us all of sunlight, fun, everything. If you're any trouble he'll put you in there and bore you to death."

"I'm going to tell him that I'll work on his treehouses, like he wants me to," said Billy. "I'll say I need to do a lot of work at the castle, making plans and things. That way I can be a nuisance, like Tweed and Fustian were at the castle. The Thumping-Jollys are going to Carillon tomorrow to ask if the Quarter Court can be moved to an earlier date before he can do any more damage. Taffeta's going to help me."

"But what happened to Jampot?" asked Drina. He was sprawled on the floor with his head in her lap, and she stroked the silky mane. "He's been healthier since he came to Twidings, even since they stopped him

going down to the lake. I thought it was just the food and water."

"I'm sure that has a lot to do with it," said Granny Annie. "And Billy told me that you'd spun Gerbil a story about needing to bath him, so I thought he needed to look bathed."

"The lion, not Gerbil," said Daffodil.

"The water supply here is pumped from the lake," said Granny. It's good water. We took him outside, washed him down with soap, rinsed him, washed him again with some frothy stuff that Veronica Thumping-Jolly uses to wash the sheep, then rinsed him down with my own nettle and marigold infusion. He enjoyed it all so much that we gave him one more washing and rinsing, and then we found the only patch of garden where the sun still shines for him to get dry. Didn't he come up well! Now, Drina, you should sleep. It's only a few hours before the train goes."

"And when you get to Carillon," said Daffodil, "you can go to my brother Tarquin. He's a student there. I'll give you his address; you could stay with him, he's terribly untidy but I suppose you could sort him out, or he'll find somewhere for you to stay, so you needn't worry about where to go, and I'm sure Tarquin—"

"Thanks, Daffodil," said Drina, still stroking Jampot, "but I won't stay in Carillon. The circus won't be very far away, so I'm going to find Ma and Pa. They need to know what's happening here. But you should come with me, Granny."

"Oh, I don't think so, Drina," replied Granny, settling

comfortably into her chair. "You're capable of going on a train on your own and finding the circus. Take the money that we meant to spend on a lake permit, in case you need to pay for a coach fare."

"It's not that, Granny," said Drina. "I mean it's not safe for you here, and I couldn't bear to think of you in Gerbil's grey room."

"Drina's right," said Billy.

"She really is," agreed Taffeta. "You should go."

"Tarquin would help you," said Daffodil.

Granny sat up straight, attempted to fold her arms, and failed because her plaster cast got in the way. All the same, she looked quite stern.

"This is very kind of you," she said firmly, "but I have lived in this village all my life, girl and woman, Copperbeech and Snapdragon, maiden and mother and grandmother too. I was married here, my children were born here, and they all know that if ever they need me this is where they will find me. I've stayed here through winters when the snow came up to the windows and stayed for two months. I've been here in summers when the lake storms were so fierce that waves came over the roofs and the mecessaries were swept away." She stopped, put her head on one side and did her lemon face. "And I will not, not, NOT be driven out by a Gerbil!"

"You could come to Thumping Old Hall," suggested Daffodil.

"I will stay *here*," said Granny, and nobody argued any more.

\*

Drina found it hard to move when Granny woke her. Taffeta, who had stayed overnight so that she could go with Drina to the station, nearly fell over Jampot when she stumbled out of bed.

Granny was fluttering about in the kitchen. "We can't have you fainting from hunger," she said brightly. "I've packed rolls, apples, biscuits, a bottle of water and some ham for Jampot, chopped up into tiny pieces so that he can manage it. Have you got his teeth?"

"I don't suppose he'll need them," said Drina, then thought again. You never knew when a lion might need his teeth. He already looked a lot more impressive than when he first arrived, but he'd look even better with his teeth in. There was just enough room to fit a set of in her bag, between her nightie and the book she was reading.

"And you'll need a large bottle of last year's elderflower fizz," went on Granny. "It's under the sink. The two of you will have to lift it between you. Don't try to drink it; it's explosive, to start the train. Nithering Day isn't charging you any train fare, so we should help with fuel costs. Put it in the wheelbarrow."

The jar was so heavy that it took all Drina and Taffeta's strength to lift it. They hurried away through the chilly morning, taking turns to push the barrow, with Granny and Jampot walking alongside them.

Drina had been trying very hard not to think about the journey. On all her visits to Twidings she'd managed to avoid the Day Train with its clanks, jolts, rattles and

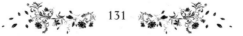

jerks. As far as she knew it had never come completely off the rails – not yet, anyway – but she couldn't see why not. That was what came of having too much imagination.

"Have you ever been on the Day Train, Taffeta?" she asked.

"Loads of times," answered Taffeta happily. "It's fun. Not when it keeps stopping, but it's exciting when it goes fast. Sometimes you have to get out and push. I was on it once when it went really fast downhill."

"That must be even worse than uphill," said Drina.

"It *was* going uphill," explained Taffeta. "Then it shot backwards and Daffy was sitting opposite me and she landed in my lap." She laughed. "She was screaming, and then it stopped really hard and we both landed on the floor. If you're lucky you'll have a ride like that."

Drina said nothing.

"Are you scared?" asked Taffeta.

"A little bit," said Drina at last.

"You'll have Jampot with you," said Taffeta. "You needn't be afraid of anything."

The train was already at the platform, with only one coach behind the gleaming green engine. A long hoot and a puff of steam greeted them and Nithering Day, with a smile on his lean face, put his head out of the cab window and waved.

"One gallon of high-strength elderflower!" called Granny, waving back. "Girls, wheel it to the engine!"

"Good powerful stuff!" said Nithering Day. "Now,

young lady, settle yourself in the carriage and strap yourself in. We'll have you out of Twidings before Gerbil Cravat gets his socks on."

There was no going back. Taffeta opened the carriage door.

"This one's got comfy seats in," she commented. "Lucky Drina."

"I'll be back soon," said Drina. "I'll find Ma and Pa, and we'll bring help." She didn't know what sort of help, but they had to do something. "Jampot, come."

Jampot sat back and growled at the train.

"Silly Jampot, there's nothing to be afraid of," said Taffeta. "Drina, he's not happy because you're not happy. You have to show him there's nothing to be afraid of."

"What if there *is* something to be afraid of?" argued Drina.

"Oh, there most certainly is," said Granny. "There's the grey sitting-room in the castle, and if you and Jampot don't get on that train that's where you'll be. And Twinkle Baggotty will put a silver ribbon round Jampot's neck, curl his mane, sprinkle him with perfume and teach him to beg for biscuits."

"Jampot, get on the train," ordered Drina, and stepped into the carriage. "If I can do it, so can you. March!"

There was just time for farewell hugs, and Drina shut herself into the carriage. She chose a seat in the middle, which she felt would be safest, and held Jampot tightly. She had just let go of him with one arm

so that she could wave to Granny and Taffeta when a bang like a firework rocked the train.

"It jumped!" she shrieked.

"It always does that!" shouted Taffeta from the other side of the window. "If you look you can see elderflower fizzing all over the..."

Drina didn't look. With a rattle, a squeak and a lurch, the train was moving, then growling, then careering up the hill in clouds of steam.

Gerbil Cravat stared down at Billy Will-do Fiddlestep, who was smiling broadly up at him. Billy had arrived at the castle very early with an armful of wood, a ruler, pencils and a knife. Green Shirts watched from every side.

"Good morning, Lord Cravat!" said Billy. "No hard feelings about yesterday. I'm really grateful, sir, for you giving me a job. When do you want me to start work? Now?"

Gerbil Cravat's eyebrows lifted. His moustache twitched. His eyes narrowed.

"I'm glad you've seen sense, Billy," he said. "In time, all this village will come round to my way of thinking. The future Lady of Lullwater will give you your instructions. I have more important work to do myself. Wait here."

Twinkle Baggotty tottered down the stairs in her tall heels. She did her little fingertip wave as she strutted over to Billy. "Hello, Billy!" she said in the soft, husky voice they were all becoming used to. "Do you know, these shoes are killing me."

"Take them off then, miss," said Billy. "Don't wear them if you don't want to."

She gave a trill of giggles and looked past him at the nearest Green Shirt, who was Wendy-Jane. "Isn't he a sweetie!" she said. "Come and sit down, Billy. Windy or Mandy or whatever your name is, tell someone to bring coffee. And orange juice. And some of those nice squishy pastries. And . . . what's your very, very favourite breakfast, Billy?"

"Any chance of a bacon sandwich, please, miss?" asked Billy.

"And bacon sandwiches," ordered Twinkle. She sat down and indicated a chair for Billy. "Now, as you know, Lord Cravat wants treehouses so our visitors have a really exciting time in the village."

"I'm sure they'll have that," said Billy. Living in a treehouse was very exciting, especially when you fell out of it. He bit into a bacon sandwich. They weren't half as good as the ones at home, but at least it was breakfast.

"I wonder if my new lion likes bacon sandwiches?" said Twinkle. "But they might not be good for his little problem. Now, Billy, the treehouses must be absolutely charming. That means that they should look just a teeny bit lopsided and patched up, but inside they must all have a large bedroom with room for a feather bed and a wardrobe, a bathroom with running water and a proper flush lavvy-wav, a comfy sitting room and a balcony. The balcony is very important so that they can sit outside in the evening sipping little drinkies

and watching the birds flying about and all the little squirrels and bunny rabbits running up and down the trees. Do you think you could put up swings? With garlands of roses?"

"Oh, yes," said Billy. "I can fix up alarm clocks too, if you like."

"Ooh, I don't know," said Twinkle. "I don't think people want alarm clocks when they're on their holly-wols."

"They'd have real little twittering birds and everything," Billy pointed out.

Twinkle clapped her hands. "How lovely!" she cried. "Can you really do that?"

"No problem," said Billy. "I'll train the sparrows. And, miss, do you think I could do the designs here at the castle? I mean, so I can show you the drawings and models and stuff and make sure you like them."

"What a professional you are!" she said with admiration. "You'll be ever so welcome." She looked past Billy at Gerbil, who had just slunk into the hall. "Gerbil, darling! Billy is going to make some dinky-winky houses for us!"

"How delightful," observed Gerbil, who didn't look at all delighted. "My dear Twinkle, would you check the menus for this week? You are so good at that sort of thing."

Twinkle blew him a kiss and left the room. When she was gone, Gerbil stepped closer to Billy.

"I have heard a most disturbing report from Harry this morning," he said. "It appears that your cousin escaped from my sitting room last night."

Billy's eyes widened. "Escaped!" he repeated. "But she wasn't in prison, was she?"

"Prison! Of course not!" said Gerbil quickly. "But she was under my protection in the castle and I am concerned that she is no longer there."

He bent down. His face was so close that Billy could see the hairs in his nose.

"I wonder," said Gerbil in a voice full of malice, "I wonder how she found her way out? Do you have any ideas about that?"

Billy shrugged. "No, My Lord. I don't have any ideas, My Lord. But that's our Drina for you. She grew up in a circus; she knows all about escaping, even if she didn't have to do any escaping because she wasn't in prison, was she? She could get out of anything. Our Drina could even get out of being protected. . ."

"But if—" began Gerbil, but Billy continued,

". . .protected in a grey room with a tiny window. . ."

"– if your cousin is not here—"

". . .with the door locked," went on Billy. "If it hadn't been so boring she might have stayed—"

"IF," roared Gerbil, "IF YOUR COUSIN IS NOT HERE, WHERE IS SHE?"

"I wouldn't know," began Billy – and then he had an idea so good that it amazed him. It could have been one of Drina's, and would keep Gerbil occupied for some time.

"I'm puzzled though," he said. "Getting out of a locked room, that's easy for Drina. But getting out of a castle with all these guards everywhere, I can't

137

understand how even she could do that. She couldn't, could she?"

Gerbil turned sharply. "Wendy-Jane!" he yelled. "Harry!"

They arrived at a run.

"Have the castle searched!" he ordered. "Every inch of it!"

"Yes, My Lord!" said Harry. "What are we looking for?"

"The Snapdragon girl," he snapped. "She must still be somewhere in the castle!"

Harry shouted orders. Soon Green Shirts were running up and down stairs and in and out of rooms.

"I'll help!" said Billy and tried to run after them, but Gerbil's hand was on his shoulder.

"Not you," he said. "I am still awaiting the delivery of a lion to the future Lady of Lullwater. Perhaps you can tell me who will bring the lion?"

Billy was saved from having to answer by Twinkle tottering back into the room.

"All the menus are super," she announced. "Dinners this week will be delishy-wish. Were you talking about my lion? Isn't it exciting?"

Gerbil smiled. Billy wished he wouldn't. "We were indeed discussing your lion, Twinkle, my dear," he said. "Billy, perhaps I should send a Green Shirt to help..."

They were interrupted by a loud and furious banging at the door. Mixed with the pounding of fists and the shouting of Green Shirts came Taffeta's tearful voice.

"Let me in!" she screamed. "Let me in, please, please, I need to see nice Miss Twinkle! *Pleeeease!*"

Billy ran to the door, but Gerbil had already nodded at a Green Shirt to let her in. Sobbing, she threw herself at Billy then caught sight of Twinkle, pushed Billy away, and threw herself at Twinkle instead.

"Taffy, what's wrong?" asked Billy.

"You poor little thing!" exclaimed Twinkle. She rocked Taffeta gently and patted her shoulder. "Tell me what's the matter. Tell Twinkle."

Taffeta hiccupped wetly into Twinkle's shoulder. "He's gone!" she wailed. "Jampot's gone!"

"Gone where?" cried Twinkle.

"I don't know," sniffed Taffeta. "He was all washed and dried and ready and I went to find a pretty ribbon for a lead and when I came back he'd gone! He must have jumped over the wall, and we didn't know he could do that. I called for him everywhere." She took out a large white handkerchief, blew her nose and cuddled against Twinkle. "Did he come here? Did he come looking for Drina?"

"Drina? Here?" asked Twinkle.

"Excuse me, Lord Cravat," said Billy. "Excuse me, Miss Twinkle, I mean, My Lady, I have to explain to my little sister." He took Taffeta's hands in his. "Taffy, you have to be a very brave little girl. Can you do that for me? We can't find Drina. Nobody knows where she is. We think she must still be in the castle, but we don't know where."

There was a brief pause while Taffeta decided who

to cry over next. She chose Billy and flung herself into his arms, and he pressed her head against his shoulder.

"Jampot's sure to be looking for Drina," he told Twinkle.

A Green Shirt ran down the main staircase and came to a halt in front of Gerbil.

"No sign of her, sir," he said.

"Why would she be here?" asked Twinkle.

"Then search again!" barked Gerbil. "I want Drina Snapdragon!"

"So do I!" came a voice from the door.

Nobody had noticed Granny arriving. She advanced down the hall with a Green Shirt on either side of her, looking very tiny between them.

"Mr Cravat," she said sternly, "My granddaughter Drina did not come home last night. I believe she is here and I demand to take her home."

Gerbil's eyes narrowed so much that Billy wondered if he could see. He glared at the guards. "Why – and you had better have a very good answer – why did you let Mrs Snapdragon in?"

"Please, Lord Cravat," said one, "we arrested her."

"You arrested Granny?" demanded Billy.

"Be quiet," ordered Gerbil. "Arrested her for what?"

The guards looked at their boots, then at each other. "Please, Lord Cravat, she asked us to," said the one who was doing the talking. "She asked to see you and we told her she couldn't, because you were busy, so she said we'd have to arrest her."

"And I suppose you'd just arrest any old lady who asked you to?" sneered Gerbil.

"No, My Lord. We told her we couldn't arrest her for nothing. And then she pulled this spiky thing out of her hair and pointed it at me."

A sound like a snarl came from Gerbil's throat. "A hairpin?" he growled. "You arrested an old lady with one arm in plaster for threatening you with a *hairpin*?"

"One of the pretty ones with a butterfly on?" asked Taffeta.

"Oh, how sweet!" cried Twinkle.

"And now that I am here," continued Granny, "I demand to know why my granddaughter is being kept in the castle. Bring her to me at once."

"What is she talking about?" asked Twinkle. "Gerby, what does she mean?"

"Your granddaughter was here under my protection," said Gerbil. "She—"

"Protection?" demanded Granny. "Who did you want to protect her from? Me?"

Billy suddenly realized that he was smiling and he wasn't supposed to be enjoying this, so he did his best to scowl. Taffeta was gazing at Granny with adoration.

"My dear Mrs Snapdragon," said Gerbil smoothly. "Your granddaughter was free to leave the castle whenever she chose, and she has done so. I have no idea where she is. In the meantime," he walked slowly towards Granny, and his face was unpleasantly pale, "that child and I had arranged for the delivery of a lion. It was to be brought to Miss Twinkle Baggotty by nine

o'clock this morning. That hour has now passed and the lion has not appeared. Failure to deliver a lion is a very serious offence."

"Oh, surely there isn't a law against that?" said Granny.

"Enough!" whined Gerbil. "You will all go to my sitting room and stay there until your mangy old lion turns up!"

"Good idea!" exclaimed Billy. "Oh, hang on, how will you find the lion if we're all locked up?"

"He can't even find Drina," remarked Granny.

"Silence!" roared Gerbil. "My Green Shirts can find the lion. Barry, send out search parties. Take a net to trap the brute with. Knock it on the head if you have to, but bring it here!"

There was another knock at the door. A purple V-shaped vein on Gerbil's forehead began to bulge and throb. Billy's day was getting even more interesting.

"What NOW?" bellowed Gerbil.

A guard opened the door. "The vicar, My Lord," he said, and in walked Benedict Goodenough. As it was a warm day he was wearing shorts with his clerical shirt and collar.

Gerbil managed a smile. "Good morning, Reverend!" he said. "I suppose you're here to talk about the wedding?"

"In a way I am, yes," said the vicar.

"Excellent!" said Gerbil. "I'm sure the future Lady of Lullwater will want to discuss music – and rings, and bells – and – and white things. I'll leave you both to talk it over."

"I'm afraid it isn't that simple," said the vicar. "I asked for your birth certificate and you haven't brought it to me. And when I've seen birth certificates I need to read the banns."

"Oh, talk to Twinkle," snapped Gerbil. "I have Snapdragons to sort out."

"Fiddlesteps," said Taffeta.

"Lord Cravat," said the vicar, and this time his voice was a little sterner, a voice that you really had to listen to, "With no birth certificate and no banns the wedding cannot take place on the date you require. Another three weeks—"

"Another three weeks will be too long," said Gerbil in a low, dangerous voice. "Remind me, vicar. Who is the Lord of Lullwater?"

"It wouldn't matter if you were the king," said the vicar calmly. "I couldn't marry you in church on that day. It wouldn't be legal."

Gerbil folded his arms. "I will be married on that day," he said. "If you refuse to marry us I'll get a special licence and we can be married by the judge when she comes to take the Quarter Court. We can have the service here in the castle, or on the Village Green if the weather is fine. Twinkle, my dear, would you like that?"

"Darling, it would be so romantic!" trilled Twinkle.

"Then you are free to do that, My Lord," said the vicar. "Good morning. I have people who need me."

"Not so fast," said Gerbil, and nodded at the Green Shirts.

"Run, vicar!" yelled Billy.

But Benedict Goodenough didn't even try to escape as two Green Shirts held him by the arms.

"Take the vicar to the sitting room while he considers his decision," said Gerbil.

Billy saw Taffeta about to run after them and caught her wrist. Taffeta hitting the Green Shirts wouldn't help. All morning she had been crying on purpose but now she was doing it for real.

Benedict Goodenough looked over his shoulder. "It'll turn out all right, Billy Will-do," he said. "No need to cry, Taffeta."

Presently they heard clicking as the door locked. Granny Annie's voice cut icily into the silence. "Now that you've locked up one of the best men in Twidings," she said, "kindly tell me where to find my granddaughter."

"Still wailing about her?" snarled Gerbil. "Old lady, I have no idea where the circus brat is, and I don't care so long as she isn't making trouble for me. But the rest of you are making a very great deal of trouble indeed. I'd tell Barry to arrest the lot of you, but up till now I have only one sitting room and no dungeons. It won't take long for me to build them though, so you had better obey me. Go, before I become unpleasant. Green Shirts!"

The Green Shirts stamped to attention.

"This tribe of Snapdragons and Fiddlesteps can go free, but watch them. And find that lion. And get my carriage ready. I can take a guess at where young

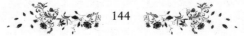

144

Snapdragon is, and if I find her, I find the lion." He glanced at Billy, Taffeta and Granny. "Why are you still here?"

Twinkle did her little stilt walk to Taffeta. "Gerbil's ever so grumpy today," she said. "It's best not to argue when he's like that. Off you pop."

Billy, Granny and Taffeta left hand in hand with their heads high.

When the carriage was ready, Gerbil put on his big black cloak and climbed in. Harry took the reins. "Where to, My Lord?" he asked.

"Carillon," said Gerbil. "I'm going to see the City Clerk and arrange for the Quarter Court judge to marry us if Goodenough doesn't see sense. And I expect to find young Snapdragon there too. Drive on!"

# Chapter Twelve

"Snapdragon Family Circus?" said the woman at Carillon Station. "They've gone to Riversmeet, and no trains go there and there won't be another coach today. If you're rich you could hire a carriage. Or you could walk, but you wouldn't get there before midnight. I suppose you're a circus girl yourself, with that lion. Does he do tricks?"

"Yes, I am and, no, he doesn't," said Drina. "Lions shouldn't do tricks."

The woman looked more closely at Jampot. "I went to Snapdragon Circus a year or two back," she said. "They had a lion then, but it didn't do much. It was old and shaggy-looking, not like this one."

Drina smiled and stroked Jampot's soft mane. "I suppose we'll walk," she said. "Can you can tell me the way, please?"

"You need to leave Carillon by the North Gate," she said. "Then turn right at the second crossroads, and keep going."

"Thanks," said Drina. "I've been to Riversmeet before, but not from here. And not..." She nearly said "not on my own", but stopped. "Not just me and my friend."

There was a waiting room on the station where she shared breakfast with Jampot and planned their next move. The Day Train had taken a long time. They had stopped once because the engine needed more grease and once because a cow was asleep on the line. In between, she had drifted into sleep.

"What do you think, Jampot?" she said. "Can you manage a long walk?"

He put his paw on her knee and looked up at her, and she was sure there was mischief in his eyes. He shook his mane and flexed his honey-golden legs.

"Of course you can," she said.

They walked in the sunshine through the streets of Carillon. It was market day, and there were stalls everywhere with people crowding round them. There were pyramids of oranges, bakers' stalls piled high, and sweets bright as summer flowers. Long rolls of patterned fabrics made her think of the Fiddlesteps. She bought an ice cream and was turning away from the stall, snapping off the bottom of the cone to make another ice cream for Jampot, when somebody called her name.

"Driiina!"

Drina jumped, dropped Jampot's ice cream, and turned. Daffodil was beaming at her. Jampot licked up the ice cream, then licked Daffodil.

"What are you doing here?" asked Daffodil loudly.

"Going to find my family," said Drina. "What about you?"

"I came with Mum and Dad," said Daffodil. "They've gone to see the judge to get the Quarter Court brought forward to an earlier date, and it looks as if we'll get it very soon, within a few days, and they'll put a stop to Gerbil building his horrible hotels and blocking out all our daylight. Mummy and Daddy are at the inn opposite the City Hall. They like it there, it's really nice, and there's. . ."

"Daffy, I can't stop," said Drina. "I have to get to Riversmeet. It'll be dark before I get there."

"We can probably hire you a horse, if you can ride," offered Daffodil. "Mummy and Daddy would pay for it."

"Thanks, but there's Jampot," said Drina.

Daffodil looked surprised. "Couldn't he just run along beside you?"

Drina hadn't thought of this, but it made sense. Now that Jampot seemed so much better, he probably could trot alongside a horse. It would certainly be quicker than walking."

"If you're sure they won't mind," she said.

They walked back through the market crowds to the inn at the centre of town. Daffodil was talking about the Quarter Court and how Gerbil would get what was

coming to him when Drina saw something that made her stop dead and clutch Jampot's mane.

"Daffy, look!" she whispered. "That coach!"

She caught Daffodil's arm and drew her into a side street, with Jampot staying close at her side. Pressed against the wall, she leaned out just a little to take a better look. "That's Gerbil's coach! It's got a hammer on the side!"

Daffodil leaned round the corner to look and jumped back, flattening herself against the wall.

"He's getting out!" she whispered. "Drina, you and Jampot stay here. It won't matter if he sees me; I'm just out for a day in Carillon with Mummy and Daddy. I'll spy on him and let you know when he's out of the way."

It was a good plan and would probably have worked, but just as Daffodil stepped out of their hiding place and Drina pressed further against the wall, a child called loudly, "Look, Mummy! That girl's got a lion!"

"Oh, yes!" said somebody else. "Look, a lion!"

Daffodil darted back to them. "He heard that!" she gasped. "He's coming. Run!"

Drina ran, with Jampot beside her. People shrank out of the way as the lion galloped past. She dodged into a side street then another and another, until a high wall was ahead of her and she had to turn into a warren of alleyways that took her almost back to where she had started. On the corner almost opposite the inn was a church with a huge dark porch and she slipped into it, hiding far back in the shadows.

"Jampot, lie down," she gasped breathlessly, and he

settled beside her. Cautiously, she peered out. People were hurrying about, asking where the lion had gone, and whether it was dangerous and (which was much the same thing) was it hungry? Daffodil was pointing towards the South Gate and telling everyone the lion had gone that way.

The inn door opened and Gerbil Cravat stormed out.

"Where is it?" he was shouting. "Lion! Where is it?"

Drina could no longer see Daffodil. People were telling Gerbil and each other about the lion, and how big it was, and that they weren't sure but they thought it went thataway.

"Harry, find it!" ordered Gerbil. "Was anyone with it?"

"There was a girl," said someone, then somebody else said that there wasn't, and another said there were two of them, and at last a shopkeeper ran from his shop to say that he was going to fetch the Carillon police force, what with it being a lion on the loose. Carillon was so big that it had two policemen, he said, and they couldn't both be having a day off on market day.

"Indeed," said Gerbil. "The lion belongs to my fiancée, and that girl stole it. If you see a lion and a ginger-haired girl, there will be a reward of..."

In the porch, Drina knelt and whispered to Jampot, "We have to get out. The whole town's after us."

Then she thought of something very simple. Probably impossible, but very simple.

The one place where Gerbil wouldn't look for her.

She stayed still until Gerbil and a lot of other

people had gone away in the direction Daffodil had shown them. Soon there was nobody about except two old women with their backs to her, looking in a shop window.

"Jampot, come!" she whispered.

In two seconds she dashed across the street and into Gerbil's carriage. Jampot jumped in beside her, and she shut the door. Strictly speaking, she thought, this was stealing. But she didn't have a choice.

The only thing Drina had ever driven before was a circus wagon with Ma or Pa on the seat beside her. Hopefully the horses would know more about this than she did. She looked to check that it was safe before slipping out from the carriage and climbing up to the driver's seat.

On the seat, which felt much too high, she picked up the reins and made the clicking noise that horses like. Then she flicked the reins and pulled a little on the left, towards the North Gate.

It was very, very late that night when Gerbil Cravat reached the castle and climbed down from his hired carriage.

Barry came to meet him. "You have a new carriage, My Lord!" he said.

Gerbil banged the carriage door. "It is not a new carriage!" he growled. "If that girl turns up here again she'll be arrested for theft of a carriage and two horses! And as for that lion, it's caused enough trouble. I want it shot!"

"But, sir, Miss Baggotty. . ." he began.

Gerbil whirled round and glared. "Don't talk to me about Miss Baggotty!" he snarled. "She's got a castle to live in! She'll be Lady Cravat of Lullwater! Isn't that enough for her?"

# Chapter Thirteen

In the circus ring, clowns tripped over each other and fell into pots of wallpaper paste until Amazonia tucked them under her arms and carried them away with their shoes flapping behind them. Sapphire and Spangle, their costumes glittering, somersaulted through the air. As they prepared for the final parade, Ma's little dog Pompom began to whimper.

"Couldn't you have gone earlier?" said Ma. "Spangle, take him out for a wee, and be quick about it!"

Drina parked the carriage behind the circus wagons and waited for the performance to end. She fetched water for the horses and took off their harness. There were plenty of people in the circus who loved horses and wouldn't mind grooming another two.

Jampot was asleep in the carriage. As soon as they had got safely out of Carillon she had let him out to run beside the horses, until she decided that he was getting tired, and let him back in.

He looked comfortable, so she left him where he was.

It grew cold. Gerbil had left one of his gold-lined cloaks in the carriage. She didn't want to put it on – Gerbil had worn it – but she needed something to keep her warm, so she put it on inside out; it was less Gerbilish that way. It had been made by the Fiddlesteps, so there was something good about it. Then she climbed back on to the driver's seat with the cloak, which was far too big, wrapped round her.

"Ma!" whispered Spangle as she ran back into the tent. "Ma, there's a lady outside! She's got a carriage and a golden cloak!"

Ma was concentrating on what was happening in the circus ring. "Whoever she is, she's missed the show," she said.

Spangle turned to Sapphire and told her instead. "Real beautiful horses!" she said. "And she drives them herself!"

Sapphire peeped out through the tent flap. She saw the tall, proud shape of the carriage against the night sky, and the gleam of the golden cloak.

"She must be very important," she said. "And rich. Spangle, we're on again after Amazonia. Get your headdress on."

Spangle put on the silver, feathery cap that Sapphire handed to her. "It's a nuisance having to sort our own costumes," she said. "It was much easier when Drina did it."

The final parade began.

Amazonia lifted men above her head and folded iron pokers into question marks. Saphhire and Spangle danced on galloping horses. The audience cheered and stamped their feet.

The Snapdragon family waved and smiled as they left the tent, then gathered to look at the carriage and the cloaked figure climbing down from the seat.

"Madam," called Pa, "may I help . . . Oh, look at this! It's Drina! Our Drina!"

In a wild, happy moment Drina was caught up in her father's arms and swung round. When she had wriggled free she opened the carriage door, and Jampot jumped down, shook his mane and rubbed his golden body against her.

"That's never old Jampot!" exclaimed Ma.

"Isn't he beautiful?" said Drina. "That's because . . . well, it's a long story."

"Is that your coach?" asked Sapphire.

"Is that your cloak?" asked Spangle.

"Er, no," said Drina and put her hands against her face because she knew she was blushing. "I borrowed them. There's a lot to tell you."

"Let's get cleared up and have supper," said Pa. "You and Jampot must be hungry. Have you come all the way from Twidings today? How's your granny?"

More than anything, Drina was tired. She'd only slept for about three hours at Granny's and dozed a bit on the train, and today she'd been sitting in the fresh air trying to get two horses to go where she wanted them to. She gave an enormous yawn.

"You need to get your head down," said Pa kindly. "Leave Jampot and the horses to me. Your old bunk's being used as a costume store so you might be more comfortable sleeping in your carriage. I'll fetch blankets."

By the time he returned, Drina and Jampot were curled up in the carriage, fast asleep.

The next day, sitting in the sun beside the circus wagons, Drina told her family about Gerbil and all that he was doing. There were cries of "that wicked man!" from Ma, and "poor Granny! Poor Taffeta! Poor Mr Goodenough!" from Sapphire and Spangle, and finally Pa said quietly, "That Gerbil is upsetting Ma. He's taking the sunshine away from my mother."

"He's doing it to everyone," said Drina. "The Thumping-Jollys are trying to get the Quarter Court brought forward so they can stop him before it gets worse. Daffodil thinks it could be very soon."

"Not soon enough," said Pa.

"And he's determined to marry Twinkle, so I think if the Quarter Court is brought forward he'll try to hold the wedding early too. I had to get out to save Jampot, but the rest of them are still there."

"It won't do," said Pa firmly. "This needs sorting out.

We've got two performances today, but tomorrow's a day off. Tomorrow we're going to Twidings."

"To do what?" asked Ma. "We can't just turn him out of his castle."

"This is the man who locked Drina in that awful room!" said Pa. "I'll drive this wagon right through his castle and out the other side! We'll get him out if I have to find the judge and drag her to Twidings myself!"

"We'll have to start early," said Drina. "It'll take most of the day to get there."

"I don't know who you mean by 'we'," put in Ma. "You won't be safe there. Your father and I will go."

"I'll be safe if you're there," said Drina.

"Can I go?" asked Sapphire.

"If she's going, I'm going," said Spangle.

Pa sighed. "We might as well take the whole blooming circus," he said. "We could always fit in a show at Twidings."

"We'll pack up as soon as tonight's show is over," said Ma. "That should give us an early start in the morning."

At the end of the afternoon show, Drina did something she hadn't done for a long time – took Jampot's teeth and fitted them into his mouth. For the first time since she had left for Twidings, she paraded round at the end of the show with her lion beside her. Afterwards she washed the teeth and hung them up to dry in the afternoon sun.

It seemed that half the circus crew had heard half

of Drina's story, so she had to keep repeating it until finally they all drifted away to do a bit of rehearsing or sorting out of costumes or having a little sleep before the next performance. Jampot stretched out in the sun and Drina rested with her head on his flank, hearing the thump of his heart.

"What do you suppose is going on in Twidings?" she asked. "It'll be evening before we get there, Jampot, and Gerbil can do a lot of damage in a day."

"From all you've said, that's certainly true," remarked Amazonia, who had come to sit beside her. "Tell me more about this Mr Cravat. Exactly what does he look like?"

"Tall, thin," said Drina, "dark. He likes grey suits and big cloaks and his voice is high and whiny."

"One sticky-out ear?" asked Amazonia.

"Yes, it is!" said Drina in surprise. "And a little moustache..."

"...that looks as if it has a life of its own?" suggested Amazonia.

"Yes!" Drina laughed. "And a way of looking at you..."

"...like a crow!" said Amazonia, and smacked one large fist into the palm of her other hand. Jampot sat up quickly in case anyone needed protecting. "Got him!"

"You know him?" said Drina.

"It was long before I joined the circus," said Amazonia. "In those days he wasn't Gerbil Cravat – he called himself Grendel Carp – but it's definitely the same man. I wasn't Amazonia the World's Strongest

 158

Woman; I was Amy Truscott from Muckleton. I was the best blacksmith around and I did weightlifting as a hobby. I say a hobby, but I won prizes, and the prize money was very good. I made more money out of the weightlifting than I did as a blacksmith. I was younger and sillier than I am now.

"Grendel Carp came to our town and opened a jeweller's shop. He did very well; soon he was making a fortune. Sometimes I'd do bits of wrought iron work for him. Then all of a sudden he vanished – just disappeared one day, and nobody knew where he'd gone. Most of the stuff from the shop went too. We had magistrates and detectives turning up, and lawyers. It turned out that his jewellery business was a great big fraud. All that gold and silver, all the jewels – half of it was fake and the other half was stolen. He'd been up to all sorts, cheating people out of their money, including me. He ran off with everything I had, and nobody from Muckleton saw him again."

"He did that?" cried Drina. "How did he get hold of your money?"

"Ha!" said Amazonia. "I'll tell you how he got my money. Didn't I tell you I was younger and sillier then? Well, he can't marry that girl from your village. He's already married!"

Drina gave a little bounce of delight. "Who to? Can you prove it?"

"Prove it?" Amazonia was smiling broadly. "I've got my marriage certificate in the wagon! He's as married to me as he was the day he disappeared with all my money

and I've been hoping to catch up with him ever since! Why wait until tomorrow? Let's go after him tonight! We don't have to take the whole circus, I can sort him out with one hand!"

# Chapter Fourteen

"Tonight!" exclaimed Ma when Amazonia's plan was explained to her. "How will you find your way to Twidings in the dark?"

"There are lamps on the carriage," said Amazonia. "And it's a full moon."

"And we're a circus!" said Drina. "We've got fire-jugglers! They can light us!"

"They'll need horses," suggested Sapphire. "Make sure they're blinkered so the fire won't spook them."

"They're Snapdragon Circus horses," said Spangle. "Nothing spooks them."

"And we'll come on after you in the morning," said Ma.

By the time they were ready to go it was dark and cold, but all the circus stood about to wave them off. Amazonia and Drina were to take turns riding in the coach and driving the horses. Food and drink for the journey had been packed and stored under the carriage seats. Two fire-jugglers were ready to ride ahead, each holding the reins in one hand and a blazing torch in the other. Jampot, Drina had decided, could do a bit of running and a bit of riding in the carriage, as he wished. She was already in the driver's seat with the reins in her hand when Ma shouted, "Stop!"

"What?" asked Drina.

"Jampot's teeth!" yelled Ma. "You left them drying! You never know when you might need them!"

Finally, once the teeth had been packed away, Drina flicked the reins and clicked her tongue to the horses. "We're going home!" she said.

All her life she would remember that journey with a thrill of joy and a lift of her heart. The steady clatter of hooves as the horses trotted briskly forward under the stars. The fire leaping into the night. The whirr and rattle of the carriage. The padding of Jampot's paws as he ran beside her. She was just getting tired when she heard the carriage window open.

"Have a break, Drina," called Amazonia. "My turn!"

Drina snuggled into the coach with Jampot beside her. He shook his mane, and they looked out of the window at the stars.

"Look, Jampot!" she said. "It's like riding in the sky. Or flying. Are we flying?"

She nestled against him and drifted asleep.

 162

The stopping of the coach woke her. Amazonia was climbing down. "Time for a rest," she said.

They were near a stream, so Drina watered the horses while the fire-jugglers lit a campfire. Amazonia made hot drinks for everyone, then it was Drina's turn to drive again. She was still tired and felt she'd much rather curl up in the carriage with a warm lion, but, not wanting to seem feeble, she patted Jampot and climbed up to the driving seat.

After what seemed like hours her hands began to feel damp, then slippery, then sticky. Her head felt heavy. Something bumped, she was falling – why was she on her back in the road? She sat up. Jampot was standing guard over her, and the fire-jugglers had turned and were riding back, reaching for the horses' bridles.

Amazonia jumped down. "You fell off," she said. "You must have been falling asleep. I should never have asked you to take that last turn. And look at your poor hands!"

Drina looked. The slippery stuff on her hands was blood where the reins had cut her fingers. She hadn't noticed it hurting before. Then she understood that she was able to see her hands because the sky wasn't as dark as it had been. The fire-jugglers walked to the stream and there was a sizzle of steam as they put out the torches. Drina followed them and dabbled her hands in the water to wash off the blood. "We've damaged a coach wheel," said Amazonia. "But that's all right. We can leave the coach here and ride the rest of the way."

*

*Thud* went Thud. Billy woke up, climbed down from his treehouse and ran through the village. It would be a busy day.

Pinned to the tree on the Village Green was a notice:

*Gerbil Fundamental Cravat, Lord of Lullwater, and Twinkle Zirconia Baggotty are to be married by Judge Agatha Steele by special licence at Twidings Castle on Saturday at noon. All are welcome.*

*Strictly no dogs*
*No children*
*No trouble-makers*

*The Quarter Court will meet at two thirty for a brief meeting on the Village Green.*

Billy glanced round to make sure nobody was watching and turned the notice upside down. Then he ran on to the wooded side of the castle where Taffeta was waiting for him under the sitting-room window with a bag over her shoulder.

"I've been here for ages," she said, giving him the bag. "I need a leg-up."

He cupped his hands for her foot, and she scrambled up the wall to the window. After a couple of shoves, it opened.

"Good morning, Mr Goodenough," called Taffeta. "Your breakfast is here. Stand well back, please, Billy's a good shot."

Billy took aim. A buttered roll flew through the window, followed by another ("Cheese!" called Taffeta), and another ("Marmalade!") and an orange.

"And Mrs Goodenough sent some books," she said. "They have to be small ones to get through the window. "And your toothbrush. Oops."

"It's hard to throw a toothbrush," said Billy.

"You might want to rub it on your sleeve to get the soil off," advised Taffeta.

"Bless you!" came Mr Goodenough's voice from the sitting room.

"Bless you, too, Father Benedict!" called Taffeta, and dropped down into Billy's arms.

"Time to get ready for the wedding."

The wedding preparations had kept the Fiddlesteps extremely busy. Twinkle wanted a wedding dress that stuck out like a balloon, puff sleeves like two more frilly balloons, petticoats, a train, an embroidered veil, satin slippers, butterfly pins for her hair and a velvet cloak to put on if it grew cold. Soon after Taffeta and Billy had served breakfast for the vicar, a procession of Fiddlesteps arrived at the castle, each carrying a parcel.

"Miss Twinkle's gown," said Satin to the Green Shirt at the door.

"Lord Cravat's suit," said Velvet.

"Miss Twinkle's petticoats," said Linen.

The procession finished with Billy and Taffeta, each carrying a prettily painted wooden box. The Green Shirts stepped in front of them.

"You two aren't allowed in here today," they said. "What's in the boxes?"

"The butterflies for Miss Twinkle's hair," said Taffeta. "And safety pins, just in case."

A Green Shirt snatched it. "I'll take it," he said. "What's in your box, boy?"

"Gold laces for Lord Cravat's wedding boots," said Billy. "And wax for his moustache."

"Leave it here and lose yourself," ordered the Green Shirt.

Billy and Taffeta walked slowly away with their heads down. "What have you done with the key?" asked Billy.

"It's in my shoe," she said. "What about yours?"

"Swallowed it!" said Billy.

By eleven thirty a crowd had gathered outside the castle, waiting to be let in. Nobody wanted Gerbil to marry Twinkle Baggotty (except the Baggottys, who had changed their name to Baggotti, to rhyme with dotty, because they thought it sounded better) but they all wanted to see what would happen. Normally Twidings people wore their best outfits for a special occasion, or even a not-special one, just for the joy of wearing them, but today everyone arrived in ordinary clothes. Some wore candle hats without candles. The Thumping-Jollys wore black except for the Honourable Veronica's pearls.

All eyes turned to the road from Carillon. Far away a carriage was rumbling slowly down it, painted deep green with gold edging and two bells on the door.

Four brown horses stepped proudly along, and at five minutes to twelve the wheels whirred to a stop outside the castle.

Out stepped Judge Steele, a tall woman with short grey hair and a stern face. She wore a green robe with two golden bells embroidered on the back, and the Green Shirts stood back to let her pass. Soon after that the people of Twidings were ushered into the great hall of the castle and were most disappointed to find that it hadn't been decorated and was as grey as ever. Granny, who had had her plaster removed the day before, flexed her fingers.

"What a disappointment!" she said. "No flowers! No music!"

"And they're late," observed Kate Applemint. "It's ten past twelve and neither of them have turned up."

Quarter past twelve came and went. The judge looked at her watch, took a book from a pocket in her robes, and began to read. Several people took out their knitting and had finished quite a few rows when Wendy-Jane came to the front of the hall.

"Excuse me," she said. Everybody looked up because it was so unusual for a Green Shirt to say "excuse me" or anything else polite. "Has anyone seen the two youngest Fiddlesteps? Billy Will-do and Taffeta?"

The Fiddlesteps all shrugged and went back to their knitting. Wendy-Jane sent Green Shirts searching for Billy and Taffeta, then ran back upstairs. There was a sound like a small wooden box being thrown across a room and hitting a wall, and she ran back down again.

"We need a butterfly hair pin," she announced. "A white one."

"I could make you one," offered Granny. "Normally it takes me about half an hour but I'm out of practice, having just had my plaster taken off. I'd have to go home for the materials. Say an hour and a half."

Wendy-Jane sighed. "Oh, forget it," she said. "I'm sure the wedding will go ahead very soon."

The judge looked at her watch again. "If Lord Cravat and Miss Baggotty aren't ready in ten minutes," she said, "we'll go straight to the Quarter Court meeting and there won't be any wedding today."

"Good!" said Veronica Thumping-Jolly.

Wendy-Jane went upstairs again.

"Well?" asked the judge when she came back down.

"Some important keys appear to be lost, Your Honour," said Wendy-Jane.

"I'm not surprised," remarked Granny. "They lost Drina."

The judge turned a few pages of her book to look ahead. "You can have until I've finished this chapter," she said. "It won't take me long."

Wendy-Jane trudged wearily up the stairs this time, but in less than a minute she was back. She disappeared down a corridor and came back with an axe.

"Oh, my word, what will she do with that?" wondered Granny out loud as Wendy-Jane plodded upstairs. Presently there came the sound of splintering wood.

"Good heavens!" said Granny. "Was that necessary?"

The judge was just putting in her bookmark and taking off her glasses when Gerbil appeared at the top of the stairs. He marched down, his cloak swishing round his grey suit and a flower in his buttonhole. His moustache looked strangely wild. Then everyone stopped looking at Gerbil because Twinkle was sailing down the stairs with silk and lace billowing round her. She did her little wave at Gerbil and for a moment her smile faltered – then she beamed again and floated to his side. The judge rose to her feet to begin the service.

A large rock stood by the side of the road from Carillon to Twidings. Anyone sitting on the Carillon side was completely screened from the village, which is why Billy and Taffeta had hidden there, stopping now and again to peer cautiously round.

"They're not out of the castle yet," said Taffeta.

"The only way they could get their stuff out of those boxes would be by smashing 'em," said Billy. "They might not have done that yet. Is there anything else we can do to hold them up?"

Taffeta thought, and finally shrugged. "I wish Drina. . ." she began, then, "Billy! Look!"

Two horses were galloping towards them. The riders rode in the stirrups and waved. Alongside them, with long strides and a flowing mane, ran a lion.

"Drina!" cried Taffeta.

It didn't take long for Drina to tell them where she'd been. She had just finished when the castle doors

169

crashed open, the Green Shirts cheered and Twinkle billowed from the castle on Gerbil's arm.

"That's that," sighed Taffeta. "Billy and I did all we could to stop it, but he's married a Twidings girl."

"Oh, has he?" said Amazonia. "I need to say hello to your Mr Cravat."

"They'll be starting the Quarter Court next," said Billy. "It's sunny, so they'll have it outside on the Village Green."

"Jampot, come!" said Drina. Jampot stood up.

"Just a minute," said Billy.

"Jampot, lie down," said Drina. He did, and looked up at her with happy eyes.

"When you and Jampot got away," said Billy, and had to swallow and start again, "when you and Jampot got away, Gerbil was livid. If he sees you, you'll be arrested, and Jampot – well, he said something about shooting."

Drina wrapped her arms round Jampot's neck. "Just let him try," she said.

"That's the trouble. He will," said Billy. "Stay here, Drina. When the Quarter Court starts, all the people who have complaints about him will line up and tell the judge what he did. Gerbil is allowed to put his side of the story and the judge will decide who's right. Taffy and I will watch and let you know when it's safe for you to come down."

"In the meantime I'm worried about your poor old vicar in that sitting room," said Amazonia. "Can any of you get me a large green shirt?"

 170

"No problem, they gave Mum one to copy," said Taffeta. "I'll run and get it. See you at the Village Green, Billy."

On the Village Green a table had been placed beside the tree and covered with a green cloth, which had been well chewed at one corner because Poodle had found it before anybody else did. When Billy got there Gerbil was complaining that the Thumping-Jollys should pay for a new one, and the Honourable Veronica was explaining that it was her own tablecloth in the first place and she'd happily pay herself to get a new one because she didn't like it anyway. There was a high-backed chair for the judge, armchairs for Gerbil and Twinkle, and wooden benches for everyone else. Barry and Wendy-Jane were in place behind Gerbil and Twinkle's chairs, and a few other Green Shirts stood round nearby. The rest of the workforce, such as the Trabbershire men, didn't have to be there, but some of them had turned up out of curiosity.

"Attention!" called the judge. "I call this Quarter Court of the Village of Twidings-on-Lullwater to order. I present to you Gerbil Fundamental Cravat, Lord of Lullwater by his purchase of the Castle of Twidings and by marriage to Twinkle Zirconia Baggotty. If anyone has any complaint against the Lord of Lullwater, you may make it now."

Dozens of hands shot up, including Granny's, the Thumping-Jollys', and all the Fiddlesteps', some of them still knitting.

171

The judge sighed. "This could be a very long Quarter Court," she said.

"One person can speak for all of us, Your Honour," said Squire Thumping-Jolly. "Mrs Snapdragon, would you speak up for the village?"

Granny Annie stepped forward. Sunlight flashed from her hairpins. From a pocket of her dress she took out a small book.

"What book is that?" asked the judge.

"It is the book of *The Lullwater Laws*, Your Honour," said Granny Annie. "And the Lord of Lullwater must keep them."

Gerbil stood up. "I object, Your Honour," he said.

"Sit down, Fundamental," said the judge. "Mrs Snapdragon hasn't said anything to object to yet. You'll have your turn. Proceed, Mrs Snapdragon."

Arriving at the castle, Amazonia strode past the first pair of guards. One of them was playing a card game against himself and the other was asleep. The axe that Gerbil had used to break into the box that held his laces was propped against a wall. Amazonia picked it up and hefted it. *Perfect.* She had listened to Drina's description and knew which corridor led to the sitting room.

But Harry was blocking it. "I haven't seen you before," he said.

"I'm new," said Amazonia. "I'm one of the special detachment."

"I don't know about any special detachment," sneered Harry. "Get lost."

Amazonia stepped back a little. "Do you know what happened to the last person who spoke to me that way?" she asked.

He didn't, so she showed him, then shouted through the sitting-room door.

"Mr Goodenough! Can you hear me? Good. Stand back from the door."

Two powerful strokes of the axe and the door splintered. One more, and there was a gap big enough for Benedict to climb out. He looked scruffy and pale, but his eyes were bright and he greeted her with a broad smile.

"Thank you so much, madam! I don't think I know you, do I?"

"Amazonia," she said. "We have to get out before this Green Shirt raises the alarm."

"How long have we got?" he asked.

"Until he comes round. Take care now, you'll have to step over him."


Granny had almost finished listing Gerbil's offences. She had started with denying villagers access to the lake and worked her way through excessive charges for passes, depriving the village of sunshine and poisoning the fish.

"And worst of all," she said, "false imprisonment. He put my granddaughter in a room in his castle and now nobody knows where she is. And he's locked up the vicar."

The judge rubbed her eyes wearily. "Lord Cravat," she said, "what do you have to say in reply?"

Gerbil began a long speech about how anyone could go to the shore if they bought a permit, and the fish numbers would soon recover. At this point, Billy decided it was time to let Drina know where they were up to. He left his seat and wove his way through the crowd and away from the Green.

"I wonder where you're going, son?" asked Gary as he grabbed Billy and clapped a gloved hand over his mouth.

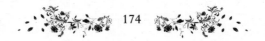

# Chapter Fifteen

Jampot had been restless since Billy left. His ears twitched. He flicked his tail, then trotted up the hill and sat staring at the fence in the direction of the lake. Even when he lay down he was alert, turning his head from side to side.

"Jampot, stop it," said Drina. "You're making me nervous. Come!"

He came to her, but would not lie down or sit still. He shook his mane.

"You're like a cat in a thunderstorm," she said. "What do you want to tell me?"

He growled very softly towards the water. Then he faced her, opened his mouth very wide and waited.

"What's that for?" she asked. Could he mean ... "You want your teeth?" He had always waited for her to tell him that it was time for his teeth. Now, he seemed to be asking for them. She took them out, smoothed them and fitted them into place.

"Good lion," she said softly. "Beautiful!"

Now that he was a renewed lion he looked magnificent with his teeth in place. Even Drina was impressed, and she'd made those teeth out of twide and old costumes. She looked down towards the Village Green, but the castle and houses screened it from view.

"I thought Billy would have been here by now," she said. "Perhaps we should go. What do you think?"

Jampot sat bolt upright and pawed at her hand. Then he turned and crouched like a stone lion on a monument.

She had seen him do that before, but not for years, not since she'd been small. He turned and looked into her eyes.

"You want me to ride?"

On the Village Green, the judge had heard the Twiders' complaints and Gerbil's answers. Finally, she stood up. So did everyone else, out of respect. It was suddenly breezy, so they turned their backs to the lake.

"The permits and charges must stop," she said. "All access to the lake must be free."

There was a wild cheer from the Twiders and a lot of jumping up and down from the children.

"And I must ask Lord Cravat to stop building," she went on. "It's causing too many problems."

"Ask?" repeated Gerbil. "Does that mean that you can't *make* me stop building? In that case, I'll go on."

"No!" cried the crowd.

"And it is illegal to lock people up in your castle," said the judge. "I will not leave this village until I know what has happened to Drina Snapdragon. And you must release the vicar at once. Excuse me? Is anybody listening to me?"

But nobody was listening to her, not any more. They were watching Jampot, great, glorious Jampot with his mane streaming behind him and Drina on his back, careering down the hill in a blaze of gold. The sight so astonished Gary that he let go of Billy, who ran to Drina as Jampot slowed down, shook his mane and opened his mouth. At the sight of his teeth everyone gasped. Twinkle grabbed Gerbil's arm.

Gerbil stared at Jampot, his mouth opening and shutting as if he were trying to speak. Finally, in a high and terrified voice, he managed, "There! Look! Snap – girl – there she is! And that beast – danger – teeth! Somebody shoot it!"

Drina bent over Jampot, hugging him. So did Taffeta, Billy, Daffodil, Granny, and a number of Fiddlesteps, and Mrs Thumping-Jolly put her arms round as many of them as possible.

"Horrible – teeth!" squeaked Twinkle. "It's going to eat all those little children and the old lady, and the dressmakers! And Mrs Thumping-Jolly, and she's an *Honourable*!"

"I thought she wanted to keep him," said Taffeta, looking up from Jampot's mane.

"Not any more," said Billy.

"But, look, Your Honour," cried Gerbil. His voice rose higher and higher. His hands shook. His moustache trembled. "There's your Snapdragon! She's safe. She's here!"

"And so am I!" called Benedict Goodenough, striding across the Village Green. "I'm safe and sound, and most grateful to the Fiddlesteps for an excellent breakfast! Good afternoon, Judge Steele! I have to inform you that Gerbil Cravat kept me imprisoned for – I'm not sure how long, one loses track of time in a room like that."

"Well, you're free now, so stop complaining!" whined Gerbil.

"Ah, but you didn't release me, did you?" said Benedict, who seemed to be enjoying himself. "This lady did."

He nodded towards the churchyard. Amazonia was marching across it as confidently as if she were in the circus ring.

"Afternoon, Grendel!" she called. "Isn't this your lucky day!"

Everything about Gerbil trembled, even his eyebrows. He turned to run, but angry Twiders stood in his way. Poodle grabbed his trouser leg and hung on.

"I really think something terribly important is about to happen," said Granny firmly, but as something terribly important was already happening, nobody took any notice.

Amazonia handed her marriage certificate to the judge.

"His name's Grendel Carp on there, madam," said Amazonia. "But you'll find it's the same miserable villain."

"How very interesting!" said the judge. She bent over the marriage certificate and put on her glasses.

"It's a lie!" screamed Gerbil. "I have never seen this woman before!"

"Do I have to prove it?" said Amazonia. "Shall I send for the witnesses to our marriage? There's a lot of people who would like to see you again, Grendel – or should I say, Gerbil. They want to know where their money went, and their jewellery. Stone-Arm Charlie's very cross with you. Big Gertie wants to know where her diamond ring went."

"This could take some time," said the judge. "Somebody bring a rope, please, we'd better tie him up."

"How much would you like, Your Honour?" asked a fisherman, and soon everyone seemed to be running from their cottages with coils of rope.

Gerbil was tied into his armchair and the judge spread Amazonia's marriage certificate on the table beside Gerbil and Twinkle's. Twinkle was weeping prettily into a lace hanky.

"You're better off without him, love," said Amazonia. She gave Twinkle a kindly pat on the shoulder and left a grubby handprint on the white, puffed sleeve.

"Everybody, stand back and give me some room,"

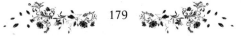

ordered the judge. "Except for you," she nodded at Amazonia, "and you, vicar."

They all sat down to watch what would happen next, but there wasn't much to see as the judge examined handwriting and asked questions in a low voice. Granny and the children began to tell each other what had happened since they last met. Several people went to the baker's shop and returned to share out picnics. Mrs Goodenough and her family brought teapots and cups from the vicarage and the Butterscotch twins fetched jugs of lemonade with bits of apple and strawberries floating in them. Everything was still covered with a film of dust, but even so, the whole event was turning into a party. Somebody found a football and there was plenty of rope left from tying up Gerbil, so there were ball games and skipping.

While all this was happening, Drina said to Billy, "What do you think will happen next?"

"Something extraordinary," said Granny. Her eyes were closed, and she looked as if she'd been sucking a lemon so long that she couldn't stop. Jampot was sitting gazing in the direction of the lake with Poodle at his side. It was unusual for Poodle to stay still for so long.

"Gerbil gets carted off to prison, I hope," said Billy.

"What about the Green Shirts?" asked Drina. "What if they try to save him? Gerbil's the one who pays them; they'll fight to protect him. It could get really horrible."

"Can we make sure they won't protect him?" asked Billy.

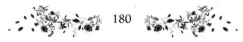

"I think I have an idea," said Drina. "They only serve him for money, so if they think they won't get any. . ."

While children played games some of the Trabbershire men joined in, Drina and Billy found empty seats near to a group of Green Shirts, who were talking among themselves.

Drina swung her feet carelessly as she spoke to Billy. "That's what I heard the judge say. Gerbil has to give all the money back; it belongs to Amazonia."

"What, all of it?" asked Billy.

The Green Shirts near them stopped talking.

"Not just Amazonia though," went on Drina. "There's all the other people he's cheated and stolen from. The coach and things will have to be sold to pay them. There won't be any money left to pay the Trabbershire men, or anyone else."

The Green Shirts hurried away. They talked to other Green Shirts. None of them looked pleased.

Billy grinned. "Job done," he said.

At that moment, Judge Steele stood up and tapped her pen on the table. Everyone stopped talking and listened.

"People of Twidings-on-Lullwater," she declared, "I believe this man, Gerbil Cravat otherwise known as Grendel Carp, to be guilty of theft, fraud and attempted bigamy, and I am taking him to Carillon to await trial."

Gerbil struggled furiously against the ropes, but the men had tied him well. The judge turned to Twinkle, who was fidgeting with her hair. "Miss Baggotty, it appears that you are still Miss Baggotty."

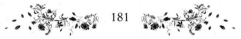

"*Baggotti!*" called Mrs Baggotty.

"Oh," said Twinkle. "Does that mean I won't be rich?"

"Indeed," said the judge, raising her voice over the growls of Jampot and Poodle.

Twinkle pouted. "Can I keep the dress?" she asked.

"Really," said the judge, "this is not the time or the place for that conversation. Squire Thumping-Jolly and the Mr Fiddlesteps, please put Mr Cravat into my carriage and lock him in. You'll have to untie him from the chair first, but leave his hands bound. And somebody keep those animals quiet!"

"Sorry, Your Honour!" called Drina, the wind blowing her hair across her face.

But she could do nothing to keep Jampot quiet. He ran to her, putting his paws up against her to demand her attention. Poodle barked furiously.

"Look!" cried Daffodil, pointing towards Thumping Old Hall. The sheep were running inland towards the Carillon road. "They're terrified!"

Billy swung himself into the swaying branches of the tree for a better view. As the men released him from the chair, Gerbil made one more attempt to escape.

"Green Shirts!" he cried. "Attack the Fiddlesteps! Grab the judge! Help me!"

The Green Shirts looked at each other and shrugged.

Gerbil was turning purple and the vein in his head looked ready to burst. "I order you..." he began, then from the top of the tree Billy shouted, "Run!"

"Lake storm!" cried Granny.

182

Jampot's growl turned to a rumble. He opened his mouth, wider and wider, showed his teeth, roared, and sprang at Drina.

She had no time to move or think. He caught her in his mouth, flung her on to his back and galloped up the hill to the castle. Everyone tore after them. Small children were caught up by their parents. With a brief "pardon me, Annie," Tam Fiddlestep picked up Granny Annie and carried her to safety. Fustian and Tweed Fiddlestep dragged Gerbil up the hill until Amazonia took over and hoisted him over her shoulder. Twinkle kicked off her high-heeled shoes and tried to run, but a powerful gust of wind lifted her balloon skirts and swept her off the ground. Benedict Goodenough followed them all, counting heads as he went.

Drina leaned forward with her hands on Jampot's shoulders, but his stride was so sure and strong that she knew she could have let go and held up her arms, like Sapphire and Spangle on the circus horses, and not fallen off. The castle doors were open and Jampot hurtled through them into the Great Hall, then slowed and turned as if to check that the others were following him. Out-of-breath Twiders stumbled in: Billy and Taffeta, Daffodil, Poodle, falling over his paws, and Amazonia with Gerbil over her shoulder. Tam Fiddlestep put Granny back on her feet. Somebody had managed to grab Twinkle's feet as she blew past, and she arrived with bits of leaf in her hair.

Drina jumped down from Jampot's back and he padded up the stairs with everyone following. At a

big landing window he settled down and Drina knelt beside him.

"Oh!" she gasped and held him tightly. "Oh, Jampot!"

They were high enough to see over the wall and across the lake. But it wasn't Lullwater Lake now. It was a raging sea, where high white waves rolled into foam and flung themselves up the beach, breaking into wild spray, each higher than the last. Nobody spoke until Taffeta said, "Granny, what's happening? You can't get waves on a lake!"

"You can on this one," said Granny. "You're too young to remember the last really big lake storm. Even your mother can't remember it. The bottom of the lake is always shifting and churning, especially in summer, and everything that's been happening here lately must have disturbed it badly. All this building so close to the water, drilling and digging, all that rubbishy stuff in the lake killing the fish, combined with some rough weather, and you get a . . . Oh, my word!"

In a rage of foam and spray, a vast wave gathered force, faster and faster. It crashed against Gerbil's new fence, frothed over the top and rushed through the gateway.

"There's another one coming!" said Drina.

Even though they all knew they were safe in the castle, people were edging away from the window. The next wave poured over the wall and rolled as far as the Village Green.

"Billy!" whispered Drina. "Granny's house!"

"Did you say something, dear?" asked Granny. "My house? My garden may get a little wet. It'll wash the dust off."

"If anyone's home gets flooded, what will we do?" said Taffeta

"We'll all help them get it cleaned up and sorted," said Drina.

"They could stay at our house till it's ready; we've got lots of room," said Daffodil.

"Exactly," said Granny. "That's the way we do things in Twidings."

The next wave was bigger, wilder, fiercer. The fence splintered. Bricks tumbled from the half-built hotel walls, with water pouring through the gaps.

Drina and Billy suddenly looked at each other with the same question –

"Where's Gerbil?"


He'd always known they were idiots. They were so interested in what their precious lake was doing that nobody would notice him. His hands were tied in front of him, but his feet were free. As the Twiders crammed against the window, Gerbil slipped away.

He hurried out from the castle by the back door that Drina and Daffodil had used for their escape. It wasn't the quickest way to the road but it would take him through the woods so he had a good chance of getting away unseen. As he ran down the staircase his eyes gleamed with delight. Amazonia had left the axe propped against a wall.

"How very useful," he muttered as he held his tied hands against the blade. "Perfect."

Rubbing the rope against the sharp edge was awkward – so awkward that he nearly cut off his thumb – but soon he was free and running out of the castle's back door. By the time Billy and Drina noticed he had gone he was deep into the woodland and wishing he had stopped to put his boots on.

When they realized that Gerbil was missing, the Twiders organized search parties. The Thumping-Jollys would lead one group to the west and the Fiddlesteps would take another to the east. Another group would go north towards Carillon. Drina, Billy and Amazonia joined the Carillon group.

"Aren't you taking Jampot?" asked Amazonia.

"I think he's had enough," said Drina. "Go on ahead, I'll catch you up."

She knelt beside Jampot, who suddenly looked exhausted. With his new lease of life, he had run and played more in the last few days than he had for years. He had galloped down the hill and up again with Drina on his back. Now he lay quietly, awake and gazing at nothing, his head on his paws.

"Jampot," said Drina gently, stroking him, "please may I have your teeth?"

He raised his head and yawned, and she eased the teeth out. There wasn't much spit on them.

"His mouth must be dry," she said. "Granny, will you..."

186

"I'll look after him," said Granny. "You go and catch that Gerbil."

Drina ran.

Hobbling and wincing in his stockinged feet, Gerbil was nearly at the edge of the wood. About time too, he thought, hating every tree, every twig and every rabbit hole. Woods were terrible spiky places where branches scratched you, tree roots tripped you up and sharp things stuck into your feet. He should have had all these trees cut down weeks ago. When he started again somewhere else he'd cut down all the trees first. He'd put up signs. NO LIONS. NO CHILDREN. And, come to think of it, NO GRANNIES.

He'd start again. He always had gold and banknotes in his pockets. He'd find another place to take over. An island might be good. He stumbled on to the road and even laughed, because every step was taking him further out of the village – just a few more paces on his sore feet and nobody would be able to see him, even from the castle. The wind buffeted him along, away from Twidings.

A whirring of wheels was coming towards him. Of all the times, there had to be a cart, or a carriage of some kind, arriving now! It could be a policeman from Carillon – or even both of them – which would be unfortunate, but if a wagon came, what did it matter? What would they see? A man in a grey suit blown along by the wind. He just had to keep going. Something flew past in the wind and caught his

eye. It was the flag from the castle with the crown and hammer, dancing away like a kite.

Round the bend in the road came two girls riding splendid horses. Behind them rolled a brightly painted wagon, and another, and another – he hobbled to one side to let them past, but one of the riders reined in her horse.

"Are you all right?" she asked.

The other rider was slowing down too. The first wagon had stopped. This was not what Gerbil had wanted, and he found he was trembling. He backed away.

The wind had swept Drina, Billy and Taffeta up the hill leading out of the village. Amazonia was harder to sweep, but she was a powerful runner and kept up. Billy reached the top of the hill first.

"There!" he shouted.

Panting for breath, Drina caught up. Gerbil stood in the middle of the road. On either side of him were Sapphire and Spangle on their horses. Behind him the wagons blocked the way.

"That's him!" shouted Drina. "That's Gerbil Cravat!"

Gerbil didn't move from the middle of the road. He was hemmed in by the riders, the circus people, those appalling children – he raised his fist in a half-hearted attempt to punch someone but the nearest circus girl seized it in a surprisingly strong grip. It was a relief, in a way, when Amazonia picked him up and threw him over

188

her shoulder for the second time that day, and carried him to the nearest wagon. At least he didn't have to walk any further.

"Would you like to drive, Drina?" asked her father. "The wind seems to be dropping a bit. Good thing too."

So Drina drove the wagon, leading the circus into the storm-lashed village, with Sapphire and Spangle riding just behind. Twiders watched from the castle. They waved and ran out to meet the procession.

Gerbil was handed over to the judge and, at last, kept under guard. Amazonia washed and bandaged his feet. "Whatever he's done, nobody should have sore feet," she said. "I like to have things tidy, and those feet are a mess."

Granny came to meet them. She looked tired and a little worried.

"All done, Granny," said Drina. "We got him. And I drove the wagon into Twidings. The only thing missing was Jampot!"

"Yes, Drina," said Granny, and her voice and her eyes made Drina afraid. "We're rather worried about Jampot."

# Chapter Sixteen

Jampot lay on his side where Drina had left him, gazing listlessly at nothing, his eyes only moving to follow her as she crossed the room to kneel beside him. She raised his heavy head into her lap. His nose was hot and dry. She felt for a pulse, but it was so weak that it frightened her.

"I gave him water, as you said," Granny told her. "He lay down, but he always does that. Only, when he tried to get up again, he couldn't."

His amber eyes were dull and his breath was shallow. His coat was still bright and glossy but in every other way he looked old and tired, and even ready to. . .

No. Drina would not think of that word. If she thought of it, it might happen.

"I'm here, Jampot," she said. "You'll get well."

Most people had gone home by now, and only a few of Drina's family and friends were left.

"Maybe he's just tired, love," said Amazonia. "He did all that running to get here, and all that roaring and galloping about today. What do you think?"

Drina didn't know. A tear ran down her face and she rubbed her cheek against her shoulder, but more tears filled her eyes and left dark splashes on his mane.

Taffeta came and sat beside her. "He's got un-Twided. Or un-Lullwatered or something," she said. "He came here all old and slow, and in no time he was running about. Remember the way he rolled about in the mecessary? Even after Gerbil took over the lake Jampot still had real Twidings-on-Lullwater food and water to keep him well, and Granny washed him with her special shampoo. All of that – the lake and the mecessary and everything – it gave him life. But he's used a lot of it up today."

"We have to get him into the lake," said Drina.

"Isn't that dangerous, after the storm?" said Amazonia.

"Not now," said Granny calmly. "The lake has done all it needs to do. You could bath a baby in there now, let alone a lion."

"Out of my way, then," said Amazonia and lifted Jampot into her arms as gently as if he were a sleeping child who must not be woken up. Silently, with Drina holding his paw, they walked to the lake.

The waves had receded, leaving heaps of wreckage all the way to the road. A jagged hole in Gerbil's wall

191

showed where the gate had been. Bricks, splintered wood and plaster sprawled over the shore line with reeds and waterweed. They picked their way through it until they stood at the water's edge. The lake was so still and so calm that it might have been a picture of a lake. As she waded in, it seemed to Drina that it had spat out all of Gerbil's changes and felt better for it.

"He'll need fish," said Billy. "I'll see if there's a boat in one piece."

When the water was up to Drina's knees, Amazonia knelt and held Jampot in the lake. Drina and Taffeta swished water over him and sang because they thought he would like that. Granny came down with all the sheep soap and the nettle and marigold rinse she had left, and they worked the foam through his coat and mane, singing and talking to him. At last Amazonia carried him back to Granny's cottage where they towelled him dry and laid him down on a rug. Granny lit a fire in the grate for him and he lay gazing at it until, just once, he turned his head to lick Drina's hand.

"You're our hero," she said. "You knew about the storm and you saved us. They'll sing songs about you for all time and tell stories about the Lion of Lullwater."

Was it her imagination or was his heartbeat stronger?

And that evening, when Billy arrived with a basket of fish, Jampot ate a little.

"I'll sit up with him tonight, Granny," said Drina when it was time to go to bed. Whatever happened to Jampot, she would be there with her arms round him.

*

She woke to the sound of Granny's laughter. Jampot bounded in from the garden, greeted her with laughing eyes and gave her a paw.

"He wanted to go out for a wee-wee," said Granny, "and I didn't like to wake you, so I let him out. I think he looks better, don't you?"

All that day, the Twiders worked to clean up the rubble from the shore. Soon there was even more of it to clear as they started work demolishing what was left of Gerbil's buildings. None of the cottages had been damaged by the storm. The mecessaries were in pieces, but Twidings people knew how to build new ones and nobody was worried about that.

A lot of the Trabbershire men stayed and helped to clear up. They'd never liked Gerbil and they did like the Twiders. Harry, Gary, Barry, Wendy-Jane and the rest of the Green Shirts had disappeared, but many were arrested later in Carillon. Several turned out to be criminals who had been on the run from the police for years. The workload was too much for the Carillon police so that the schoolmaster and the vet had to become temporary policemen.

Twinkle Baggotty spent a morning crying because she wasn't going to be the Lady of Lullwater any more and an afternoon crying because she wouldn't be rich. Then somebody reminded her that she could stop pretending to like Gerbil, and she felt a lot better after that. She didn't want to stay in the village though, and went back to her job selling dresses, somewhere even

further away than Carillon. She kept the wedding dress, and nobody minded.

The lake had washed itself clean. The fish came back. The reeds would soon grow and sunshine reached the gardens again. After a few days of clearing up, everyone felt ready for a party.

Tables were set out on the Village Green. Bunting was hung from shops, cottages and trees, and there was music from the Fiddlesteps, the Butterscotches and the Goodenoughs, and anyone else who could sing or play. There was dancing, children played, and the circus provided jugglers, acrobats and Ma Snapdragon's dog Pompom.

Taffeta watched Sapphire and Spangle with wide eyes. "I want to learn that!" she said.

Jampot's teeth were handed round and admired. Everyone said that Drina was "good with her hands" and Granny added that she was pretty good with her brain too. "She has ideas," she said, "and imagination."

"Too much imagination," said Ma.

"Impossible," said Granny.

The party went on as long as anyone wanted to sing and dance. Taffeta learned to do handstands, Daffodil tried juggling, and Drina danced down the road with Granny Annie. At about midnight Billy worked his way back through the woods to his treehouse and Drina, Pa Snapdragon and Jampot took Granny home. They sat round the fire with hot chocolate and Jampot sprawled on the rug with his head in Drina's lap.

"Well, Drina," said Pa, "Granny's better now."

Drina bent her head over Jampot. She had known that, sooner or later, somebody would talk to her about going back to the circus. Her voice came out much more faintly than she meant it to.

"I want to stay," she said. Into the silence that followed, she added, "Jampot needs to be here for his health, and I can't leave him."

"I wondered about that," said Pa.

"Mm," said Granny thoughtfully.

"I love you and Ma," said Drina. "I'm so happy now that I can see you again. But I don't like circus life. I'm no use there – I know, I can do costumes and come up with ideas, but I can't perform. I want to stay here and read books and go to school with Taffeta, and learn how to make things out of twide and work the lake."

"Your ma and I have talked about that," said Pa. "We've missed you too, and it's not just because you mend the costumes and think of all your bright ideas. We've missed *you*, Drina. But we want you to be happy."

Drina stopped stroking Jampot's mane and sat very still while she thought.

"It's like this," she said at last. "In winter the circus doesn't do much, and we have to find somewhere to stay. So why can't the circus spend the winters in Twidings? And when you come I'll be here to meet you, because Jampot and I will be here, living with Granny." She realized that there was one thing she hadn't thought of. "If it's all right with you, Granny."

And Granny laughed.

*

It turned out that Gerbil's story went back a long way. Police from all over the country were interested in him. Before he was Grendel Carp he had been Claude Fungal Gobb and had lived in another country where he was wanted by the authorities for selling gold mines that he didn't own in the first place. He had married a woman there too, and she was now behind bars for stealing diamonds.

Amazonia said that she didn't want him back, but she did want him tidied away somewhere so that he couldn't do any more harm. Gerbil was put in prison and made to repay the people he'd cheated. The Trabbershire men were paid, and so were the Fiddlesteps, for all the clothes they'd made.

At the end of the week, the circus rolled away with the whole village coming to wave them off.

"See you in November!" called Ma, waving from the wagon.

"Keep practising your acrobatics, Taffeta!" called Sapphire.

Drina shed a few tears after they'd gone, but then she made Jampot some new teeth and helped to rebuild a mecessary, and felt better. And in the evening she sat on a rock on the lake shore with her feet in the water and her arms round Jampot. The air smelt of grass, reeds and the freshness of the lake. "This time," she said, "it'll be all right. We won't have to leave, ever. You can swim as much as you like and eat all the fish you want. And I can learn to work the twide the way Granny does, and read every single

book in the house and every book in Thumping Old Hall."

Jampot sat beside her watching the fish, the tip of his tail flicking. The fading sun made the lake glow with gold, and a breeze hushed and whispered through the reeds where Billy and Taffeta leaned from a boat and pulled up fresh wet stems. Jampot shook his mane and sprang down into the water for a swim.

"You really do have good ideas," she said, and she waded out to join him. It was time for a swim in the shining Lake of Lullwater.

Look out for more by
Margi McAllister

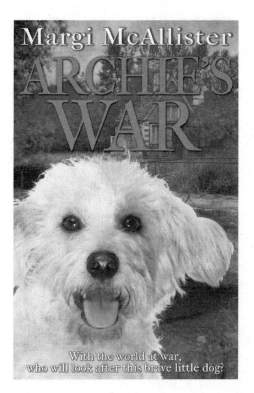

When Master Ted goes to fight at the outbreak
of World War One, it falls to Archie to look after Star.

Archie has always thought Star was a complete
nuisance, but before Archie knows it, an unbreakable
bond has grown between them. And soon Archie and
his dog go on an adventure like no other...

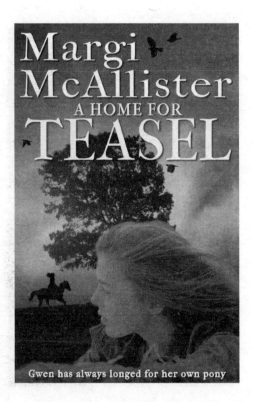

Gwen has always longed for her own pony

Gwen has wanted a pony for as long as she
can remember. When she is asked to help an
elderly neighbour, she can't believe there's a pony
that needs looking after too!

Spending time with Teasel is everything Gwen has
ever dreamed of, and more. But she doesn't realize
her love for Teasel will take her on an adventure
like no other.

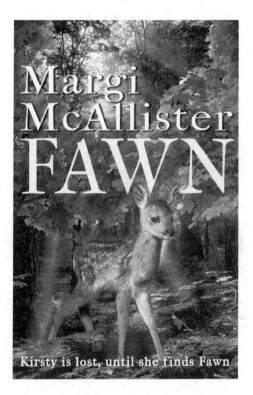

Kirsty is lost, until she finds Fawn

When Kirsty rescues an abandoned fawn, she has no idea how she will care for him – or keep him a secret. All Kirsty knows is that he needs her, and that without her help, he might not survive.

But the fawn isn't the only one who needs Kirsty. And this isn't the only secret she's keeping.